STUPID

c r i m e s

DENNIS E. BOLEN

ANVIL
PRESS

VANCOUVER

Published by Anvil Press
P.O. Box 1575, Station A
Vancouver, B.C., CANADA
V6C 2P7

CANADIAN CATALOGUING IN PUBLICATION DATA

Bolen, Dennis Edward, 1953–
    Stupid crimes

    ISBN 1-895636-01-9

    I. Title.
PS8553.043S7 1991   C813'.54   C92-091004-1
PR9199.3.B64S7 1991

Sections of this book have appeared in *sub-TERRAIN* magazine and have been read on Vancouver Co-op Radio.

Cover Design: J. Lawrence McCarthy

Printed and bound in Canada.

Barry Delta Knows People Who Are Dead.

This is not a social-work concept, or an irony, a metaphor or a joke. Under his blotter Barry keeps the patchy line of differently-yellowed obits, exactly one for every year he's been in the business.

Nine dead parolees. Enough to line up out of his office and down the hall. Enough to fill two mid-sized cars. Nine racks of faded bones, dead; shot, stabbed, beat to death, burned, over-drugged, overtaken and done.

When Barry thinks about them, which is sometimes, he tries to remember exactly how they all went, and has found this difficult. Difficult, because Barry would have had to investigate, dig around, prepare a report for the Parole Board. But with the time that has passed and the insignificance of some of them, it gets harder and harder to factor in his mind what happened.

Some of them Barry is sad about. Some of them, for various reasons, he could spit on their graves.

(Barry to Janice one night; edge of drunkenness):

And I never forget . . . I mean, I can't imagine what it's like to be locked up. Claustrophobia. I'd probably crack. But I make a point, when I go to interview, to have the guards sometimes just take me to wherever the guy is and put me in the cell with him. And go away. Not lock the door, that would be too realistic, but walk away down the tier so I can hear the footsteps fading with the echo and feel the solidness of the walls and the floor and the ceiling. Smell the sweat and the dirty toilets and all the metallic smells and the hopeless sounds of the place and imagine what it would be like to live your life here. I do it once in a while. To remind me. Every time I give up on a guy and put the warrants out on him this is where he ends up. I try not to forget . . .

1

What we have is the image of a child being mistreated: be it through incest, threatening, cruelty, burnings, beatings, torture or neglect. It is catastrophic violence in any form. This is the solid matter which forms the deposits in the soul, which corrodes and poisons, and makes the ordinary air un inadequate life-sustainer. To some it will be possible to bury; others will bleed from the start and won't stop until they're white from it. What is certain is that they will make others bleed, practically everyone they touch, and some will be children, and so the circuit will go . . .

—Prof. J.G. Prosyst, A Primer of Correctional Theory, New York: Street Fighter's Press, 1975, pp. 68-69.

Barry Delta, his friend John, Dapper Perkins and a bunch of others, burst out of the supervisor's office and quickly strode, all of them, down the hall and dispersed without a lot of talking. They sprang-stepped, moving faster than you get used to seeing civil servants move. They all frowned.

Barry Delta frowned the most. He followed hulking John into the old man's office and slammed the door behind them. John plopped into his swivel chair and reached for the phone. "How many you got?" he said, leafing through a telephone index, not looking at Barry.

"Two. Maybe just one. Depends. That's not the point."

"What's the point?"

Barry looked at the ceiling, putting his hands deep into his pockets.

"Fuck me . . . "

John dialed the phone. Barry went to the window. It had rained during the night. The streets were steaming in the June morning sun. A brightly polished late sixties model car emerged from the underground parking and flashed by. "There goes Dapper," Barry said.

"Why not? And what the hell are you doin' standing here? Hello . . ? Jerry? Yeah, gimme Jerry . . . " John cupped the phone.

"Know where they'd be?"

"Yeah, probably . . . "

"Well, get out there."

"Yeah, but . . . What about our necks?"

"T'hell with that . . . Hello, Jer? I gotta talk to you. Yeah. No. Stay put. Don't come down here. No. For chrissakes, no. Stay there. Never mind, I'll tell ya. Don't. There's a warrant out for ya. I'll be there. Ten minutes."

John hung up. Barry stared out the window. He shrugged, folded his arms on his chest and leaned against the wall.

"I dunno . . . " Barry said.

"You don't, huh? Well, I'll tell ya. The thing has happened and you gotta do something about it. 'S'what you get paid the big bucks for."

"Yeah, yeah . . . "

"Quit whining, boy." John struggled up and got his jacket. "Get out there." John left the office and lumbered off down the hall.

Barry Delta went to his office and reached for the phone.

A machine shop, working, whirring and smelling of heavy oil and hot metal wasn't the kind of place Barry expected to typically be at nine on a given morning. But here he was, picking his way through the hooded figures blazing sparks from machines, moving with their backs or the tops of their heads to him so that they could not see him. He felt a danger in that. Barry walked carefully to the rear of the shop, where a man about thirty leaned on a broom, watching him.

"C'mon," said Barry to the man, motioning with his head.

"What's up?"

"Your ass. Come on."

Out back, standing in the alley, Barry looked around before speaking.

"Lookit, Steve, don't panic, but there's a warrant out for you."

"What?"

"It's complicated. I'm doing what I can."

"What the hell's goin' on?"

"I'll give you the short form. You know how you got released that time back east and then you screwed up and went on the run for eight months and then turned yourself in out here?"

"Yeah."

"You did something like ten more and got turfed out on your statutory remission and you got by rights about . . . what? 'Nother year to go?"

"Right."

"Well, they got this strange case back east, see, a guy called Squeeg. Went to court, tried to fight the way they calculate sentences. I don't know exactly. Anyway, he beat the thing and they gave back a lot of stat remission to guys who'd been on the run at one time or another and then got caught. They had to let a bunch of guys go a little earlier than usual. So, to make a long story not a long story, the only trouble was the government appealed and got it overturned."

"So what does that mean?"

"That means that a lot of guys have been let go this last two years that they've been fighting in court who now have to be re-processed under the old system and a lot of them owe

10

backtime, so to speak. They're taking a lot of time off a lot of guys. Some not so much. Like you for instance. You only owe twelve days."

"What?"

"That's right, pal. You got out twelve days earlier than the latest Squeeg Ruling says you should have."

"Well . . . That's fuckin' bullshit!"

"I'm with you on that. Really."

"Twelve days. Fuck me. I'd lose this job."

"I hear you."

"Aw, shit . . . "

"Correct."

"Aw, c'mon, Barry. Whatta we gonna do?"

"I dunno. There's one or two things I might try but you gotta lay low. It's a good thing I don't keep my paperwork up to date or they'da scooped you this morning."

"Fuuuck . . . "

"You got a place to go?"

"Well, I dunno."

"Where's your old lady?"

"Buggered off last week. Got hot about something. Went down to her folks' place."

"Where's that?"

"Lynden."

"Washington?"

"Yeah."

"Hmmm. Anyplace else?"

"Nowhere. I'm broke, man. 'Less *you* wanna slip me some cash."

"Forget it. We gotta think, here."

"This is the shits, Barry."

"I know, I know. You think I don't know it's the shits? You're only one case. We got lots like you."

"What's gonna happen to them?"

"They can take their chances. Some of them got it coming anyway, save us the trouble."

"Well, why are you helping me?"

"Aw, I dunno. We go back a long way, I mean, you even took me out to your dad's farm and all kinds of cute stuff like that. You're okay. More okay than most. Stand-up crooks like you are hard to find. And besides, I figure you work a little longer in this place you'll be set up fine. Hate to see good work go bad."

"You're a hell of a guy."

"I know . . . Look, can you square it with the boss if you disappear for a few days?"

"I'll give it a try."

Steve took off his coveralls and went to the back office.

They drove in Barry's Honda across town to get Steve's stuff.

Steve came back to the car with a black garbage bag, partially filled, closed with a twist-tie. He jumped into the front seat, swinging his bag into the back.

Barry started the car. "Where to?"

"I can't think of a place. Can't you put me somewhere?"

"Not if I don't want the parole board down my neck. I'm supposed to be arresting you, not helping you lam. In fact, I don't even know where you are right now, and you never rode in this car. Remember that."

"Right."

"It doesn't matter where you go, so long as you're not where anybody can find you and you're near a phone and can call me in a few days to find out what's happening."

"Whatya gonna do?"

"Nothing. This is the type of bullshit that somebody rescinds or repeals or calls a big mistake or otherwise admits that somebody else screwed up and boobed somehow. Nobody'll take responsibility, but a crowd of guys'll probably convene a meeting and go to Ottawa for a week over it, complete with travel budget allocations, a banquet for two hundred, and ten dollars a day incidentals whether they spend it or not. Then they'll strike a committee to issue a report about the whole bollix and after eighteen months write a two hundred page pile of steaming horse shit that says nothing I'm not telling you right now, and cost the suspecting tax-payer several cool hundred-thousand. Meanwhile, you'd have served your twelve lousy days, lost your job, been let out to try and do it all over again and maybe screw up just because of the pure frustration and criminal stupidity of it and nobody'll give a shit about you."

"Except you," said Steve, smiling.

"Except me. Now where should I take you. And make your mind up fast, we're both hot properties just sitting here."

"I really want to see my old lady."

"That's pushing it. Hiding you until the heat's off is one thing. Getting you south of the border, out of the country, illegally entering the United States, that's a biggy."

"Just drop me at White Rock. I'll walk across."

They drove south. Barry drum-pattered his fingers on the steering wheel, nervous.

"You got phoney ID?"

"No. I'll do it somehow. Done it before."

"If you're in a car, they don't check you, just the driver, and I'm not a heatbag. Just yet, anyways."

"You don't have to."

"Might as well. No point going halfway and have you grabbed at U.S. Customs and add an out-of-supervision-area infraction to the list."

"You're the fuckinest PO an ex-con ever had, Barry."

"Yeah . . ."

There was a twenty-minute line-up at the Blaine crossing. Barry sweated, even though a breeze from Boundary Bay cooled the car. Steve lounged, relaxing, and enjoyed the water view and the far off coastline on the American side. "Last time I was through here," he said cheerily, "I was goin' the other way with a full load of weed."

"Yeah, well . . . No repeat performances, please."

The Customs Officer asked them their citizenship and sent them through without a second look. Barry stared at his rear-view mirror for longer than it was safe to drive. Nobody came after them.

Barry swung the Honda down into the border town and parked in the first available space, on a street full of porno theatres and liquor stores.

"Thanks man." Steve reached for his bag.

"Okay, look. Call me in a couple of days, see how things are going."

"Right."

"Should only be a week or so, we can sort things out."

"Fine."

They paused, Barry looked heavily at Steve.

"Behave yourself, boy."

"Don't worry."

"And not a word if things go wrong."

"Don't even ask, Barry."

"I know you're okay."

"No sweat."

"And look, if there's an emergency, like after hours, I'm carrying the beeper this month. Call anytime and I'll come get you."

"That's good to know."

Steve got out of the car and slung his garbage bag over a shoulder. "So long."

"Say hello to what's-her-name for me."

"Okay, see ya."

Back through Canadian Customs there was an even longer wait, and Barry had time to think of the mad thing he was doing. Not only that, he'd forgotten to get an address or phone number for Steve's girlfriend. What a fuck-up. Barry scowled, the car was idling raggedly, overheating, and his mind was not on his work. His mind was definitely not on his work.

What was really on Barry Delta's mind was a woman. One that just might fit the bill this time. He'd met her at a high school he'd given a Social Studies talk at. She was the teacher. A student asked:

"Do you guys carry guns?"

Barry answered, "No."

Then the kid asked, "Do you get a nice car?"

Barry answered, "No."

The class tittered, the policeman Barry was sitting beside chuckled, and Barry noticed the pleased interest in the teacher's eye.

v v v

On their first date they went to Wreck Beach, doffed clothes and swam together. They drank a bottle of wine, and when it was dark held hands on the struggle up the steep trail. She laughed often, and took few things seriously. She cared about a lot of things Barry hadn't thought about. Her eyes were large and deep. He found it easy to look into them when he spoke to her. She braided her hair and drove a Volkswagen van. The way she shifted gears, like an expert, attracted him greatly. Her name was Janice. Barry couldn't wait to make love to her.

v v v

Coming back from the beach, Barry sat sideways in the VW passenger seat, watching Janice drive, the breeze blowing her hair.

Barry half-yelled into the wind and motor sounds. "Freeze the moment, freeze my life, make it come back to me again and again and never go away . . ."

"You're a funny one," she said after a moment, glancing sideways.

"Funny or not, I can see your grin and the air on my face is so good and it's the way I feel."

"Are you often like this?"

"Only when I'm loving every minute."

"Can you do that? Isn't there anything not right? It can't be perfect."

"Yes it can. The right second. The right sight. The right amount of wine in my tummy. The trick is to hold onto it."

"Hmmm. I can't say I disagree with you. But you're unusual. Definitely unusual."

"You must be too," Barry said.

"Why?"

"I like you so much."

"I don't know what you mean."

"You must. I sense it . . ."

After a moment she said: "You tend toward presumptuousness."

"That's what they say."

"I don't wonder, what with your approach."

"What's wrong with my approach?"

"It wouldn't work with most women."

"Most women."

"Yes."

"Pure and direct, with an ample glimpse of animus. I'm not afraid. It wouldn't scare off the good ones."

"Speaking of glimpses, do you always take your first dates to Wreck Beach?"

"It wouldn't scare off the good ones."

"No. But it could disappoint some of them. I mean seeing all there is to see. They might make a decision based completely on looks."

"Hey! I feel a gratuitous slight coming on here . . ."

"No, no . . ."

"If you don't like what you saw, just let me off at the next corner. I'll catch a bus."

"I probably won't do that," she said, driving.

Late in the afternoon, John came into Barry's office and plopped the electronic pager onto the younger man's desk.

"Here's the goddamn beeper. Good luck to you."

"Thanks."

John paused at the door. "Find your boy?"

"Uh huh."

"Get him away somewhere?"

"Yup. Stuck my prick out a mile. How 'bout you?"

"Mine doesn't stretch that far, at least not anymore. But yeah, I took some chances. Shouldn't be too bad, though, I hear some other jailbird has taken the thing back into court."

"Probably reverse it tomorrow and then all of this shit was for a lousy twenty-four hours."

"Well, hope they do it before the weekend. I hate comin' in on the weekend."

"Yeah, fuck, the weekend . . ."

John grinned. "Sounds like you got something on. What's her name?"

"Old man. You're more like an old woman."

"When I was your age I didn't have time to sit around places like this and jaw to just anybody about what I was doing. I went out and did it. I had more little gals running around than I could keep count."

"It's not like that anymore John. You have to keep it down to one at a time. And you have to listen to what they're saying . . ."

"Really got her spurs in, eh?"

"Her name's Janice. She's terrific."

"Good boy. Give her a go once for me."

"John, you just don't get it . . . "

ᴠ ᴠ ᴠ

But later that night, sitting on her living room carpet, sipping wine, Barry felt like it. Bad. She asked him about his work. He tried to answer without gazing too intently at her folded legs, close in front of him on the floor. He leaned back against a pillow.

"I guess I never developed any sort of ideas or strategies or anything. Didn't even study it in school. I took English and History."

"You're just a natural then."

"Well, I suppose you could say that, although I don't know if there is such a thing in such an unnatural situation. I mean, think of being in charge of at least thirty of your fellow earth creatures, with the responsibility and power to observe them, make judgments and commit them to detention all based on your own instinct and sense of what's right. It's heavy. There are lawyers in this country who can't get to sleep at night thinking about all the power we have. There's no judge or jury, just us."

"It is scary . . . "

"More than you think. It's a good job but it's a dead end. Only the good people stay, the bad people get promoted. It's discouraging. Burnout sets in. You get pissed off at the world, and forget not to take it out on the nearest parolee. Bad things happen."

"How have you lasted ten years at it?" Janice reached out and ran a hand through Barry's hair. "And you're still so . . . nice."

"Like I said, it's a good job . . . "

Janice leaned over and kissed him.

Later, after many kisses, Janice said: "I suppose we could make love tonight. I feel very good about you. But maybe we could just leave it and enjoy the knowledge that we will for sure and that we'll probably be doing it for a good long time over and over and that there's plenty of time for it. What do you think?"

"Fine," Barry said.

"What are you really looking for in a woman?"

"Like you."

"That's not an answer."

"I'm looking for someone who's not worried about her perm."

Janice chuckled, fingering her braid.

Early Friday afternoon word about the Squeeg ruling hit the parole office. The Court of Appeal overturned the Supreme Court decision and re-established the previous *status quo*. Barry and John stood over the fax machine as the news came in.

"Right on time," said John.

"Yup. That's the thing about fuck-ups in this business. You can set your watch by 'em."

John tugged the paper from the machine. "And we're the best fuck-ups in the business, right Barry?"

"Speak for yourself, old timer."

The two men met later at the front door. Both were leaving early, John to go collect his low-laying parolee out of hiding now that the coast was clear. Barry wanted to get home early to get ready for his date with Janice. Steve hadn't called from south of the border and, rather than worry, Barry took it for a good sign. Things must have been going good. And his mind, as usual, was on other things. Tonight, he knew, was the night.

A few days with his ex was, Steve found, more than enough to remind both of why they were not still together. On that Friday night, the troubles came to a roaring crescendo with the recurrence of his bad table manners, something his ex found irritating beyond endurance. It had always bugged her when he left the table for the bathroom in the middle of a meal.

Steve had searched his mind, and was sure he would not be similarly offended if she had occasionally left the table mid-meal for the necessary interruption. A man was a man, and he had to do what he had to do.

At any rate, she threw a plate at him.

He knew it wasn't just his manners that had her riled. She wouldn't stop talking about the long-distance phone bill she'd have when he was gone again. Yesterday he'd tried to call Delta several times, and didn't feel safe leaving a message with the receptionist. From then on, his ex and her mother frowned whenever he sat by the telephone, whining out loud about long-distance charges. He tried not to get angry, trying even to forget that he'd spent most of his pocket cash on their week's grocery supply.

As the crockery sailed past his head, Steve had an unexpected rush of well-feeling, a release. This was finally the end. He could leave now with no afterthought, no guilt and no doubt. He dodged the plate, stepped quickly to the irate woman and swept her into his arms.

"Goodbye, baby," he said.

He walked the two miles to I-5 and thumbed a ride north.

ᴠ ᴠ ᴠ

A pickup stopped for him and as Steve slammed the door and the truck gathered merging-speed on the entrance ramp, the last rays of a beautiful sunset lanced horizontally upon Barry and Janice. They sat on her couch, just returned from dinner.

Relaxing, Barry belched, pepper sauce coming back to him. He tried to cover it with a cough but Janice was alert. He thought he could see his crimson reflection in her eyes.

"You said something?" she asked, smirking.

"Must have been a thought, trying to get out."

Janice laughed.

Barry drew his hand along her leg and touched the hem of her cotton skirt. He pondered, wondering if the time was now. His body-pressure rose and stopped his thinking. He wrung his jacket off and flung it across the room, onto a chair. It slid to the floor. Barry kissed Janice. His mind was not on the pager, inside the jacket, it's call button now nudged into the 'off' position by its impact on the floor. His mind was on other things.

v v v

Steve tried to call Barry, pouring a dollars' worth of change into the pay-phone for three minutes talking time. He left a message with the answering service, giving the number of the telephone booth. He bought two hotdogs and a soft drink and camped beside the booth for five hours, until past midnight, when he sensed that Barry would not be getting back to him that night. He used his last money, nine dollars, to sit in a porno theatre. Around three in the morning the projectionist turned the sound down so that the six hunched men in the seats could get some sleep. Steve got a few hours but woke up feeling more tired than when he'd drifted off. He lurched into the aisle and walked out of the theatre. Later, walking along, squinting in the early light, surprised at the sleep hard-on he'd grown and fingering the few quarters left in his pockets, he craved coffee.

He found a place that gave large styrofoam cups for cheap, and loaded up on sugar and cream. Sipping, he wandered in the fresh air, the coffee steaming in his face, across the street, past some shops and gas stations, toward where the town ended at the water. There was a beach. Steve walked a bit and sat down on a log.

From here he could see the stone cairn marking the start of the Canadian beach. Maybe a quarter-mile away. Less than ten minutes' walk, leisurely. Much quicker if you crouched and darted. But he'd heard of the patrols. He'd heard of underground

21

sensors and dogs and bad-assed border police and he believed what he'd heard. If he was going it would have to be legit, through the gates. A walkover. It would be hairy but he'd do it. He'd done hairier things before. The prospect of excitement made the morning air more welcoming. The coffee tasted better as he got to the bottom of the cup.

He waited until the sun was high, heating his forehead, and the ambient sounds of the beach were corrupted by the low rumble of what he knew was standing traffic, cars lined up on both sides of the border.

∨ ∨ ∨

Barry Delta turned the beeper back on when he discovered it, under clothes, the next morning. He and Janice were heading to the beach, and he slipped it into the back pocket of a pair of shorts. They packed a picnic basket with brie, bread and cheap Spanish champagne and headed out. The sun shone perfectly as they skidded down the trail, the perfume of new flowers on the brush making the air heady. Barry felt drunk. The night had been hot and alive. He watched Janice descend the trail, elated at the curve of her neck and the way her hair fell over her shoulders. Life was good.

They doffed, lay for awhile in the sun, talking, then decided to take a walk and a swim. Barry tossed the shorts onto the blanket and walked hand-in-hand with Janice toward the water. After a while they decided to tour the shoreline and joined a game of volley-ball. When they got back to the blanket the tide had just reached it, wetting half, dampening the picnic basket and destroying the beeper, eating its circuits with salt water.

∨ ∨ ∨

Steve strode past the American Customs complex, trying to look like he belonged where he was, and where he was going.

Through the grassland of Peace Arch Park, where families were picnicking and children played. It all felt like a scene from a travel brochure.

He tried not to sweat, but felt beads forming on his forehead, under his hair. It was the weather, turned summer-hot in the noon-day brightness. His heartrate was fine; there was pulsing, but no pounding, in his ears. He felt fear, but not too much. Just enough to put the proper edge to things. He was pleased at this feeling, knowing he had all his faculties trained and focused. It was an alive feeling he had begun to forget, working on the end of a broom in the machine shop.

He checked the surroundings, sweeping the area with his eyes without overtly glancing around. All was normal, no one looked at him with more than idle disinterest. Ahead of him the concrete path toward Canadian Customs narrowed away from the park and became more businesslike as it paralleled the clogged road.

Approaching the multi-gate entrance to Canada, Steve eyeballed ahead for clues as to how foot-crossers were handled as opposed to vehicle passengers. He identified a doorway, just off the path, and from three hundred meters away began to make out figures inside the building. He watched closely, slowing his step, as a couple entered the building, stepped to a counter, and were interrogated by a Customs Officer. He stopped as they began searching in their packs and in pockets for ID. That was it. There was no way he was going to be able to do it walking.

He crouched, untying and retying his shoelace, thinking. He was far past the picnickers, so it would look suspicious to pretend he was just out for a stroll. There were shrubs and trees across the multiple lanes of traffic, and what promised to be dense bush farther off. The cool darkness of it looked too good to ignore. Steve stepped off the curb and strode quickly amongst the cars.

There was more park-like grassland at the other side, but then, down in the thickening shrubbery, a nasty wire fence. Something you couldn't see at a distance, but very real up close. It was camouflaged so well in the greenery that Steve did not know it was there until he bashed his forehead into it in his haste to disappear into the thicker woods beyond. He knew his eyebrow was cut and would show blood. Bad sign. Things were going seriously wrong. He scrambled about and found it was not too high, meant to discourage casual walkers but not the kind of thing to retain someone determined to pass through. He clambered over the rusty wires and all but stalled in a profusion of small vines and weeds that made walking impossible. He had to crawl a distance until it thinned out enough to allow a sort of crouched walk. Making his way, he heard a siren go off, not like a police car, but like an old-fashioned air-raid wail. In his scratchy progression through the growth, Steve was only mildly awake to the fact that he might be the reason for the noise.

Deeper in, and in a clearer stretch where he could almost walk normally, Steve heard voices and commotion back at his entry-point in the fence. Quickening, he found a rough pathway, followed it, leaving the voices behind, and came to a small creek. On the other side, an easy slosh through ankle-deep water, was the back yard of a large house. He plunged across, hurried up the lawn and passed swiftly by the ground-level windows. He did not look to see if anyone watched him, and tried to be nonchalant when he hit the sidewalk and came into the view of other homes on the block. Wiping the spot of drying blood from his brow, he strolled as quickly as he could, back toward where he thought town was.

Even with wet feet, he did not attract attention and was soon back sitting on the log he had occupied all morning.

Time to think.

v v v

On Wreck Beach, Barry was shaking the water out of the pager, switching it on and off, not hopeful that it would work.

"Is it important?" asked Janice.

"Kinda . . ."

∨ ∨ ∨

Hitchhiking was out.

For miles around there would be a concentration of cops and border security looking out for just the type of loose-looking drifter he was. He could think of no friends he could entice south of the border who had a car. Trying the walk-through again was out of the question. He had to get Delta down here to pick him up, it was that simple.

Bumming a dollars' change was harder than he thought it would be. Blaine was a busily transient town. Nobody seemed to know anybody else. Suspicion appeared to be the attitude of choice. He had some luck with a drunken fisherman, and picked up the rest from the sidewalk outside of one of the town's many barn-size liquor stores.

He jabbed the touch-tone buttons, praying he'd get through.

The phone rang twelve times, then a disinterested voice answered: "Correctional Service . . . "

"Put me through to Mr. Delta please."

"We can page him. Can you leave a number?"

This again. Steve gave the pay phone number and hung up, looking around for a good place to park himself. The time was two-fifteen p.m.

Around six o'clock, a cool breeze kicked up off the water and by seven Barry and Janice were shivering, drinking the last of the champagne. On the trek up the darkening trail, Barry worried about the sodden beeper, and resolved through the wine-haze to call the answering service as soon as he could. At seven thirty-nine he was given Steve's message, and immediately called the number. He let it ring thirty-five times. Nobody answered.

One thing Barry could do was to ask the telephone company where the pay phone was. Then drive down and take a chance on seeing Steve somewhere near. It was past eight o'clock, darkness approaching. The drive would take the better part of an hour. Janice was in her kitchen cooking up a spaghetti sauce. The smell of garlic was like a drug.

But it would be the right thing to do. The numerous fuck-up possibilities ran through his head.

Janice came from the kitchen and poured him another glass of wine.

v v v

It had clouded up over Blaine and threatened rain. Steve had had to move at a little after five because a Highway Patrolman stopped for coffee across the street. Steve knew enough not to look at the man, even from this far away, but he could tell that he had generated interest.

The cop paused, closing the door of his cruiser. Steve noticed the way he walked, slowly, looking around, and the tentative way he opened the door of the diner. Steve got up from his bench and moved casually down the street. When he got to an alley, he ducked into it and walked briskly, thinking about his next move.

If the cop was genuinely interested, as Steve knew he was, he'd do something the minute he noticed Steve was gone. That pretty well blew it for staying in this town. Fuck! Things were really getting out of hand. He was stiff from sitting around most of the day. And there was something else, something that made his steps hard on the dirty pavement, made his eyes narrow and his breath short. He was angry. The hunger pains in his sides did not help the situation. The smell of frying hamburgers from down the street brought him near a rage.

v v v

He found what he was looking for after an hours' walk. This type of countrified landscape was perfect for an unoccupied house or cabin, with just enough space and trees around it to keep

26

neighbours from detecting an unauthorized entry. Though he was an armed robbery specialist, the old B&E skills, learned from the teen years, never left. He found a partially open bathroom window around the back, stepped up on a piece of lawn furniture, and squirmed through, landing in the bathtub.

He made a careful patrol of the house, entering each room cautiously, listening for breathing. No one. An absence of fresh food in the refrigerator told him the place was probably not being used. This being Saturday night with no one around, it made sense that the people weren't going to show for the weekend. Just in case, Steve opened the back door and made himself familiar with the quickest escape route.

There was canned food. He heated himself some chili. In a high cupboard over the sink, he found the booze, an almost full bottle of dark rum, some gin and other bottles. He sucked a large shot from the rum. The burn down his throat felt good and he drank some more. Later, eating and drinking at the kitchen table, he noticed car keys hanging from a hook by the door.

He stared through the darkness to the back of the property. He thought he'd seen a shed of some sort, but couldn't be sure it belonged to this place. Finished eating, he lurched with bottle in hand through the back door, fumbling for a light switch. Before he found it, he thought better, cursing himself for the lapse in judgement. Such an easy way to get caught. He tried to remember if he'd seen a flashlight. Rummaging, he found one in a kitchen drawer.

The shed was at the extreme back of the property. A rutted path lead to it. Through the padlocked doors, Steve could see an old but well-preserved pick-up truck. One of the keys on the ring fit the padlock. Things were looking up. He opened the doors, walked with the flashlight pointing to his feet, stepped around a lawn-mower and got into the truck. It was his kind of vehicle. The seat felt good on his back. He could hardly wait to get going, but knew he was too drunk by now to give it a try. He looked at his watch. Twelve-twenty a.m. A foolish time to hit the border.

They'd be looking out for drunks, with a line of police cars parked on the other side waiting for tip-offs. Better to stay, finish the rum, get some sleep, and do it in daylight.

He took a good pull on the rum. Something in the rear-view mirror glinted with the slight movement of the flashlight beside him. He took the light and pointed it behind him. On the gun-rack there was a twenty-two calibre, single shot rifle, the type used for shooting rodents and tin cans. Below it, hanging from its trigger-guard, was a .357 Magnum short barrel.

Handguns. Out in the open, where people could see them as you were driving along. Steve chuckled aloud.

America. What a country.

v v v

Barry called the answering service just before midnight. No more messages. He called again when he and Janice woke to another glorious beach-day. He called again just after brunch in Stanley Park. No word. He gave up on the beeper, and kept calling all day on the hour, hoping for the best.

v v v

Steve wrapped the pistol in a clean rag and tucked it under the passenger side of the seat. No matter what you could get away with in this country, he was not going to drive a truck with a dangerous-looking firearm swinging in the back window. He wasn't about to throw it away, either. He had hoped he'd given up playing with these things; during the long night of drinking and nervous sleep, he'd put the thing out of his mind. He'd resolved to lay the gun on the workbench and leave, the rifle too, and not complicate things.

But he found ammo in the glove compartment, and the feel of the cool metal in his hand cleared the cobwebs of his hangover instantly. It made his arm feel solid, like it had extra bone. His skin felt dry and comfortable. He could swear there was extra power in his legs. Goddamn! He promised himself he wouldn't get any ideas, hiding the gun under the seat, but it would bring a firm three hundred in the bars of Vancouver. Too good an item to pass up.

The border was more crowded than the day before. It was just before noon when Steve rolled up to the Customs booth. His gut tightened, ready. The officer looked at Steve with disinterest. A scruffy-looking hay-seed in a grimy tee-shirt, slouching at the steering-wheel of the universal vehicle of his class. Steve worked at making his face slack, no expression. He looked the officer in the eyes but did not focus.

"Citizenship?"

"American."

"Where you going?"

"Surrey."

"How long?"

"Few hours."

"Anything to declare?"

"Nope."

That was it.

Even as he checked the rear-view for cop cars, Steve knew he was clear. And there was that feeling again, rumbling down the freeway at 70 miles per hour, as fast as this heap would go, he felt the renewed power in his body that successful bad-behaviour always brought. And with a first-class piece of machine steel under the seat yet, and not a cop in sight, and nobody even knew the truck was stolen. That thought stopped him a little. Unreported or not, a truck with Washington plates was going to attract him some attention once he got to the city. Especially if some cops saw him who might have known him from before. There were still a good many of those.

He parked the truck on a side street in Marpole and, bundling the .357 down the front of his pants, boarded a city bus for home.

No matter how good it felt to get away, it was nice to be in a town where you had a valid transit pass.

That night Barry and Janice went for Greek food. Though she was having a wonderful time, and the weekend was floating by in a pleasant daze, Janice was concerned with Barry's growing preoccupation. Finally she asked: "What's the matter?"

"Nothing. Why?"

"You keep fading out on me and you go away and make phone calls all the time."

"Well I have to . . . work, you know."

"Of course I know, and I think it's wonderful the dedication you bring to your job, it's a real turn-on for me. You wouldn't believe the men I've run into who had no interest at all in any kind of work. Or the ones who have no other interest and ignore everything else. You're nicely in between. But if there's something that's got you worried you should share it with me. I want that."

"Aw, it's nothing. Just this guy I was thinking about yesterday."

"Should you maybe go look for him?"

"I wouldn't know where to start. It's a tough one, and we might as well forget it. It's out of my hands."

"Then for goodness sake leave it and come back to me."

"I like the sound of that."

Janice smiled. Barry tied into his souvlaki, trying to take her advice. It wasn't easy, but as the retsina flowed, he made it.

Food was the factor, with all the others, that tipped it to final disaster. Steve was starving, sitting in his bare apartment, penniless. If he still had a job, payday would be at least four days off. In the meantime, welfare would probably turn him away because he was employed, and he didn't like that route anyway. The last time he'd been to the welfare office, the indignity of it,

30

standing in line with all the other losers, he'd gone right out and knocked off the first bank he could find, cashing his cheque later in the week when the robbery money ran out.

Now, it was a lonely Sunday night with nothing to eat. And nothing to his name but a stolen handgun wrapped in a stolen tea-towel sitting in the freezer compartment of his empty refrigerator. He tried not to think about it. He tried to avoid it. Calling Delta was out now that there was something else in the room, waiting in the refrigerator. Something far more dependable. He tried putting other things in his mind. He went into the bathroom and tried to jerk off, but couldn't think of anyone who turned him on. Thinking of his ex old lady just made him angry. He washed his hands and walked to the kitchen. Just for a minute, let's hold it. Let's hold it just for a minute.

The metal, even freezing cold, accepted his hand like a friend.

∨ ∨ ∨

He rode the SkyTrain out to Burnaby, his pants bulging. The plan was to be a man again, to feel good about himself and get something to eat. To get some self-respect. He walked through the darkening streets and found the gas-bar he'd been looking for, a place he'd stopped at a few months ago. It was a good place for a cheap score because it was so close to the highway. It was also close to the bus-line and if a guy was to put an hour of planning into it, gauge when the bus would be coming, pull the score, keep cool and leave when your hundred-thousand dollar public transport vehicle came to get you, well, it just might be okay. There were deep woods nearby in case anything went wrong.

Steve waited an hour. The street was wide and straight. A bus every twenty minutes; he could see them coming from a kilometre away. He watched them stop; four times on average. Almost three minutes to get to him from when he could first see them. At eighteen minutes past the last bus, when he could just see the next one, he crossed the street, walked past the convenience store at the far end of the gas lot, lingered for a second while a customer signed a credit card receipt, and squeezed in the sliding door of the cashier booth.

Without a word he pointed the gun between the eyes of the teenaged boy at the till. He kept the pistol as low as possible, almost to the counter. There was a large sign laminated to the arborite below his gun-hand. It said: "After 8:00 p.m., Cashier Has Less Than $35." Steve felt relaxed and in control. He had time to think of what thirty-five dollars would do for him right now. A lot. The clerk's eyes were round and dark-looking. Steve smiled at him.

"The money, please."

"Yes, sir."

The kid reached under the counter and came up with a fistful of bills. Steve accepted the money with his free hand.

"Thank-you. I'm going now. You won't follow me, will you?"

"No."

"That's good. Just for safety sake, though, please lay down on the floor."

"Sure."

"Thank-you."

The clerk dropped out of sight.

Steve stepped out of the booth, pocketing the money and holding the gun close to his waist, looking up the road for the bus. He saw it, coming quickly to his stop.

He took one step, began to conceal the weapon, and heard an ominous click off to one side. He swung the gun in the direction of the click. A burly middle-aged man stood outside the door of the convenience store, a shot-gun in his hands. Steve noticed his uniform, like a fast-food worker. He did not think of anything else, but pulled the trigger of the .357. The shot destroyed the glass door behind the man. At the same instant, the shotgun went off and Steve felt a shock of wind as the load flew past his face and shattered a gas-pump behind him.

Steve took cover by the cashier booth, firing twice as he moved. He heard more glass shattering and smelled gasoline. He heard the shotgun being cocked again. He tried to hear the footsteps he knew would be his only clue to what was happening next. He mostly heard glass and the approaching diesel bus. Then a feeling, slight vibrations from behind him. He moved forward and whirled to his feet. The man stood beyond the cashier booth, the shotgun levelled at him through the glass. Steve shot in the direction of the man. The shotgun went off, shattering glass in the booth. A piece of glass hit Steve on the chin. He pointed the gun blindly, trying to see in the flying glass and gunsmoke, and fired twice more. He yelled aloud, shooting, and felt confident.

The man with the shotgun was no longer standing. Steve, crouching, looked around the side of the booth and saw him, prone between two gas-pumps. Steve rose, walked swiftly to him, mindless. He kicked the shot-gun away and looked down at the man, who was breathing quickly, eyes wide, clutching at emerging blood from a shoulder wound. Steve checked his gun. No more ammo. Then he remembered he had a bus to catch.

He thought for a moment about the problem of blood on his face. In the semi-light, near darkness, people might not notice. Running across four lanes of traffic, he stuck the gun out of sight in his belt, tried to wipe his chin and think at the same time. From behind the bus, a car without lights emerged at high speed, could not avoid him, and struck Steve's foot as he was running, spinning him around. Then he was on the roadway, his foot at an odd angle to his leg, just beginning to hurt. Cars were coming. He knew he couldn't move.

The bus, driver oblivious, pulled away.

v v v

As the pain in Steve's foot set in, approaching cars slammed on their brakes, making much noise. A nearby RCMP cruiser responded to a 'shots fired' report. Janice worked her way down

Barry Delta's naked back, nibbling here, kissing there. When she got to his buttocks, she opened wide and bit, hard enough to get attention.

"Teacher!" Barry shouted.

After the hospital, Steve was taken to the remand centre. Barry came to see him, sitting in one of the tight nightmares they called interview rooms. Steve was led in, limping with a cast. The guard left. The two men sat silent for a moment. Barry said: "Nice of you."

"Huh?"

"Nothing about the south-of-the-border stuff. Just the gunplay. Nice of you."

"No sense you going down too."

"Nice of you."

Silence again. Barry tried to think, tried to figure an approach, couldn't, and finally said: "Can you characterize it? I mean, is there one thing or a few things that you think might be at the root of the problem?"

"What do you mean?"

"I'm trying to make some sense of this."

"What for?"

"There has to be something, something in what happened, what you did, what happened to *you*, that tells us something. We have to take something from this experience."

"I can't think that way."

"I guess that's part of the problem. But something's got to give. There's got to be some change."

"I never thought of it."

"Well for chrissakes start! You can't go on like this."

"Why not?"

"Don't be stupid. You won't be young forever. You'll start cracking, you'll get old and pissed off, you'll turn into a bug sooner or later."

"How can it change?"

"Think. THINK! Plumb the depths. Come up with something to work with . . . "

v v v

Steve, relaxed until now, trying to keep it that way, started labouring. He began to think against his will. If Delta was good at one thing, Steve knew, he was good at not letting you go without giving something, waking you up for maybe just a second, even if you didn't want to and were determined not to. He was good at that if nothing else.

His thoughts along Delta's line were there, he'd had them but never told about them. But there was something else now. Anger. A feeling he didn't want to feel because there was no sense, within these walls, feeling it. Anger was precious and should not be spent frivolously talking to one's PO, who could not really do anything for you. But even these thoughts were intrusive. He stopped thinking. His ankle was throbbing. He shook his head. "Naw . . . " he said. "It's too stupid."

"Don't be afraid. Tell me what's in your mind."

"Forget it . . . "

"I don't have all day but I'm gonna sit here anyway. Talk."

"I . . . "

"Come on, come on."

Steve was tired of looking at Delta's darkening eyes. They wouldn't look away and even when he looked away he knew they were still there. His mind started again, and he tried not to think about all the failure, the shit, the death and the future that was hurting him bad. His cell, five floors straight up in the concrete building started to seem welcome. He winced with the pain in his leg. He closed his eyes. How to get rid of Delta? He opened his eyes. Barry was still sitting up straight, glaring into his face.

Steve decided to give Delta the next thing that came into his head. Anything to get him to leave. He concentrated. At the same instant, he knew he did not have to concentrate. If Delta wanted the truth, however inconsequential and impossible to change, then he could have it.

Steve said: "I hate my father."

"What?"

"I hate my father."

Delta slipped into daydream. Why did it take everything a new girlfriend had to give? He thought about the beach.

v v v

"Well," said Steve, "how's that?"

"Uh . . . ," Barry returned, "you hate your father."

"Yeah."

"Okay," Barry said. Steve said nothing.

Together the two men sat, feeling the jail sounds.

v v v

Consequently, given the subliminal problems, the hidden and unconscious pains, the dysfunctions will become manifest in many different ways. One may not necessarily act out in criminal ways. Crimes of excess, impulse, ignorance or omission may occur without attraction of law-keeping agencies or any type of penalty at all, save for the inevitable ravages of guilt perhaps experienced in the occasional periods of lucidity . . .

—*Prof. J.G. Prosyst, p. 108.*

2

My mother used to say to me what the hell am I going to do with you?

And Mr. Delta said the same thing the first time I seen him. He didn't say it like my mother though, he just leans back in his squeaky chair and goes tsk tsk. Smiling away. And he points to this stack of files and says not much of a criminal, huh, Wayne? Twelve convictions. From stealing donuts to picking flowers on the City Hall lawn.

v v v

He says something smart like there's crime everywhere so how come I haven't got into it and I ask him what the hell do you mean by that? He says Wayne, you just got out from serving your third bit for penny ante small-time crap that a real crook would bite his tongue and not talk about. Like, a guy wouldn't admit he'd been thrown in the joint on a three year bit for breakin' windows in a gas station and taking fifteen bucks in quarters from the pop machine. I says to him you had to be there, Mr. Delta, I was really pissed off at the guy who ran the place. And he says Barry, please call me Barry, so I figure we're off to a good start, him and me, but then he starts with all these goddamn conditions.

∨ ∨ ∨

Not supposed to drink. Not supposed to get found in bars. Not supposed to hang around with friends from the joint. Not supposed to own a car until he says. What kinda bullshit is this? I says. He says the Parole Board let you out on those conditions, you wanna go back just gimme the word and you'll go back. I says No, I don't wanna go back. I'm never going back. Fuckin' eh, I says to him. He says, that's the spirit, Wayne, now all we gotta do is find a way of following through, easier said than done.

∨ ∨ ∨

He's one for sayings, that Delta, always got a good one handy. Anyway, after that he says the best way would be for me to get a job and he's got something in mind right now. We go out of the office and ride downtown in that little piss-pot Honda of his and we pull up to this car wash. He goes to the office and I see him talking to a guy. They come out and the guy asks me some questions, talks to Delta some more and turns back to me and says no funny stuff. I says no funny stuff back to him. Then he says fine, come in at ten tomorrow and that's that, I got a job.

∨ ∨ ∨

Delta drops me off at the Sally Ann and says once I'm set up more I can look for a better place to stay. Great I says cause I'm kinda choked about staying in a place like that because what am I, a rummie?

∨ ∨ ∨

After a couple of days the boss at the wash gives me an advance and I go and find a place with these other couple of guys that work there and we all have a couple of booze-ups and get laid and life starts to look kinda good. Delta meets me downtown one time and buys me a burger and asks how I'm doing and we sit there talking like two ordinary guys, you know, with nothin' else on their minds but having beer and getting chicks and stuff. So things are going okay and I tell him I got a place and he asks me who with and I tell him a couple of guys from the wash and he says is that wise? Have you checked things out? And I tell him, hell, these guys work with me, they're not from the joint. Okay, maybe one of 'em did provincial time on a B&E or something but that's goofy kid stuff but Delta says remember what you're in for, that's far goofier than B&E and look where it got you. I says well what the hell am I supposed to do, anyway? And he says just watch yourself, you gotta be squeaky clean, cleaner than clean, way more than anybody else because you still got a year of a sentence hanging over your head. I said I get the message and he says good and the rest of the time goes fine and in a couple of weeks I'm working more hours and they seem to be trusting me around there.

v v v

But then the trouble starts when the weather starts getting good. God the sun starts shining and you just don't wanna go to work, you know? And the snobby piss-ass pansies in their BMW convertibles and Porsches with sunroofs and nice stereos and some of the nice looking chicks they'd have! Fuck me!

v v v

So I'm gettin' kinda pissed off with working during the nice weather and the boss wants me to put in more hours just when the beach season is really gettin' going. Besides that he's really buggin' my head with his bossing around and stuff and the guy really thinks he's hot shit 'cause he's got this rebuilt '61 'Vette that looks real sharp and he's got this chick who's got a pretty nice ass.

39

I mean the guy's a fuckin' wimp because his old man even bought him the car wash, he didn't even get it himself.

v v v

So I'm getting sick of everything and I meet Dickey downtown one day. Dickey and me did time one year at Forestry Lake and he was a stand-up guy in those days, I don't know about now, the fuckin' guy fools around with junk which has never been my scene, it turns you into a goof as far as I'm concerned. Gimme a good old-fashioned beer any day. Anyhow, Dickey says hey man, howya doin'? I say not bad, fuckin' eh! I been working and got money in my pocket! So it gets goin' like that and pretty soon we decide to celebrate and go to the beach.

I gotta go to work but I say to hell with it and we go to my place to get this big plastic cooler I found one night in an alley and I change my clothes to some shorts and a tee-shirt. As we're checkin' out I start wondering about leaving my leather jacket around there. I mean, you can't trust these fuckin' guys one bit and I seen one of 'em eyein' my jacket one time and it's the only thing I got that's worth half a shit so I decide to wear the thing, even though it's hot out. I figure we can sit on it at the beach.

v v v

So then we go to the liquor store for some brew and we get a sack and a half into the cooler except there's not enough room for the last two so Dickey and me drink 'em in the alley behind the liquor store and Dickey says yuck, man, warm beer and I say we'll fix that, follow me. So I lead us across the street to this Chinese grocery I been in before and we go to the back where they've got this old-fashioned pop cooler with all kinds of ice in it. I tell Dickey to keep his eye on the old Momma Chink that's minding the store while I just scoop us some ice.

v v v

So I start doing it but no sooner than I get started old Momma is down beside us looking with those black beady eyes of hers and she makes growling noises at us and waves for us to get out. Dickey kinda laughs and I try to ask the old lady if we can just have a couple of scoops of ice but the old broad doesn't speak English I guess or pretends she doesn't but just shouts some gobbley-gook stuff and points to the door. I say to her okay you fuckin' bitch we're going but here, have one 'a these, it'll cool you off and I grab a pop and slam it on the floor real hard. The pop explodes all over mine and her shoes and Dickey starts chuckling real hard and I say c'mon, let's get out of this fuckin' place and we start going but the lady starts shouting real loud and I hear guys in the back answering her and I says whoa! Let's get out of here!

v v v

I boot it with the cooler to the door with Dickey behind me and just as we get to the front I hear Dickey yell and I turn around and he's lying on the floor holding his head. The old lady is standing there with a baseball bat. Then two guys run out of the back and one of 'em has a meat cleaver in his hand and he stands there looking at me with it and the other one runs around me and shuts the door and locks it and pulls down the shade.

v v v

I mean, all of a sudden it's dark in there and it's getting scary with this guy with his giant blade staring at me and the old woman is still yelling gibberish. Then the guy who closed the door points to the mess on the floor and says you pay. You pay. You pay. Over and over and the guy with the blade starts getting closer and closer even though I can see he's scareder'n rat shit the guy, he's quaking like a fuckin' leaf but the old lady still has her baseball bat and she don't look like she's scared 'a nothing so I figure I got to do something fast.

v v v

Dickey is sittin' on the floor holding his head and saying aw, man, aw man over and over and I don't figure he's gonna be good for much. I'm still holding the cooler so I push ahead into the guy with the cleaver and dump it at him and then I run past Momma and the other guy into the back and duck into this half-open door that turns out to be the can and I slam the door and lock it.

I look around and find a wastebasket to throw through the window in there and I hear one of the guys yelling and running around but they don't try to get me and then I figure the guy yelling is talking on the phone. I get the basket through the window and ease myself out trying to be careful not to get cut because the easiest thing for the cops to do is look for somebody who's bleeding.

v v v

When I'm in the alley I start walking fast for the street and then I decide I might as well cross and keep going up the alley to get as far away as possible before I try to slip into the crowd. Then I get this idea that I should act like a jogger because they're all over the place and it would be a good way to get going quicker away from there so I start jogging but then I think I've got to get rid of this jacket because who ever heard of a jogger wearing a black leather jacket? So I take it off while I'm running and drop it into a garbage can where I know I can find it later and I come out to the street and start running down the grass part beside the sidewalk acting just like your average physical fitness type.

ᐯ ᐯ ᐯ

I turn a corner two blocks up and right there is a cop sitting on his motorbike watching for people doing left turns and I just run past with an innocent look on my face and he just watches me go by. I hear his radio going but think nothing of it but then I hear him start up and pretty soon he's riding beside me and he says okay, pull up a second, sir.

ᐯ ᐯ ᐯ

So I pull up, there's nothing else to do and I figure he's just gonna ask me my name or something because he's being real polite. So I just stops and says what can I do for you officer? He gets off the bike, looks at me funny and says first off, you can stretch out on that grass there with your arms and legs wide apart. I says Hey hold on a minute, what's this all about? And he just puts a hand on my shoulder and tells me to do as I'm told. Later on a couple of cars come and a grand total of five cops are standing around me on the grass. Then they take me to the back of one of the cruisers and I yell over at the motorcycle guy, I says, how did you know it was me?

He says I could see it on your face, kid, and besides, you just opened your big mouth and told me.

ᐯ ᐯ ᐯ

See it on my face, he says. Like fuck! Bullshit! Musta got a description on the radio or something. So here I am and they're charging me with wilful damage and assault. Assault! Who had the fuckin' knives, anyway? Son of a bitch! I'm fighting those fuckin' Chinks all the way on this one I'll tell ya, I even told my lawyer I wanted them charged with unlawful confinement or something like that. Says he's gonna look into it.

v v v

And Delta, he waits his sweet time to come and see me. Almost two weeks before he drags his ass out here and then he just smiles and sits back and starts again with that snarky crime in the street crap. To paraphrase, Wayne, he says to me, some people are born to stupidity, some people have stupidity thrust upon them. What the fuck're you talkin' about! I says to him. Talk straight for a fuckin' change!

v v v

Now, Wayne, he says. But I says to him para-faze-up-your-ass! Jesus Christ! and now I'm in this fuckin' joint for who knows how long and everything's gone to shit. Two days pay at the wash I'm not gonna get. Lost my leather jacket.

v v v

I says to Delta, I says what the fuck is going on? You guys are supposed to help people like me. But he just shrugs his shoulder and writes some notes in his book and goes away.

v v v

Sometimes I wonder what the fuck a guy keeps on going for, I mean why? There's gotta be something they can do for you.

I'm starting to think like that all the time. I think this I think that. I can't stop. That's what this place does to you, drives you crazy.

I think of my mother and how she always said what am I going to do with you? Well yeah! What? Fuck . . . . What do you do with a guy like Delta?

Barry Delta Has Glimpsed Madness.

Yet, he would be wise enough to say, he has not seen *all* of madness. Only someone completely sane would be foolish enough to say they had.

3

It's a political thing, this sex business. The guys who get all the pussy are the smart ones, the rich ones, guys with the educations. The political ones you see on television. I'll bet they get fucked so they can't stand it anymore. Nice pussies standing behind them when they talk to the cameras, I'll bet they been done by the best there is. That's what this sex bullshit is all about. Who needs it. We all make our adjustments. My adjustment is a well-picked location; a dead time of night; soothing words, I'm basically a good guy at heart, never hurt anybody; and a blade wrapped up in my pocket. A blade. Wrapped up in some underwear. A pair of panties if I can get some. With the proper instruments you can do anything. Like a blade, a word, perfectly tuned, like my expensive digital watch. Perfect. It's perfect.

v v v

"Okay, the name is Delta. Barry Delta. I'm your PO."

"Mr. Delta, I . . ."

"Barry. And you're Stanley? Do you use Stanley?"

"Yes. I want you to understand. I will be no trouble."

"Hold it."

"What?"

"Hold on here. I was just reading the file. Five women . . ."

46

"I've been through that, Mr. Delta. There were more. I've self-disclosed that."

"How many more?"

"Two."

"For a total of seven."

"That's right."

"You self-disclosed."

"Yes."

"Who to?"

"The doctors. The group inside. You, now."

"You went to the group."

"Yes. I found it good."

"You did. That's great. Tell me, what's different this time around? I mean, this was your first bit. You were . . . let's see, twenty-nine when you went in. You're thirty-seven now. You've got four years left on supervision. What's different now? How are you not going to rape women?"

"I have a good perspective on that, Mr. Delta. I know a lot more about myself. I feel badly for what I've done. But there were female nurses in the hospital there, I got to know some of them quite well. I never had that before, female friends. I feel like I can handle myself better now."

"Meds?"

"Yes. Lithium. Sometimes thorazine. Plus valium for the first month or so. They gave me a carry at the gate. Don't worry, they're only twos. Ten a week. So I won't be out there selling the stuff or going all goofy or anything."

"I'll be seeing you later this week. Maybe twice. Everything goes fine you'll only be in here once a week to pick up your pills. Or better yet I'll come to you. Got a place yet?"

"No sir. I thought I'd get started after I saw you."

"Okay. Go ahead. Gimme a call when you know where you'll end up. See you in a couple of days."

"Okay, Mr. Delta. And thank you."

They give you that bug juice so they can control your thoughts. You see, the average man in prison for sex crimes is really a special, politically dangerous person that the government can't afford to have walking around because they know too much. Guys like Delta make me sick. All they do all day long is make sure we take the drugs that make us less of a threat to the government and monitor all the robotics they have to watch us. When I found this place it took me half a day to de-bug it. There was stuff all over. Good thing I quit taking the drugs. I'm still not clear yet but I had enough smarts to find all the stuff they put in here to keep an eye on me. By tomorrow I'll be clear enough so I'll be able to figure out how they knew I'd take this particular place of all the places in the city. They must have some incredible mind-control equipment, machinery people don't even dream about. Or maybe they've got the whole city bugged! Unbelievable!

v v v

I have certain energies within me, like a liquid. It feels like thick oozing gasoline that burns in the middle of my chest and flows downward, all the way, until my power is bared and ready like a sword. When I'm off the juice long enough . . . man! Can I feel the burn! The problem is I've got to have a target. A target worthy of being a target. It can't be just anything. It has to be good. If I don't use the energy, if I don't blaze my sword, bad things happen. The liquid starts to congeal and fester like mashed-up spiders in my insides, sick and awful, and I will vomit and go crazy. My blade goes dull and will not operate, even to let out those other poisons the government put there. That's what life is like for me. A constant fight to control my power, keep myself alive, and carry on the struggle against those who would control me.

v v v

"Hiya Stan. This your address?"

48

"Yes, sir. I was lucky. Fifty-five a week and only three sharing a bathroom. It's much better than before."

"You seem different. Anything wrong?"

"Nope."

"Nothing bothering you?"

"Things are just fine, Mr. Delta."

"We can't force you, but you can get counselling. Even a doctor if you want. Just give me the word."

"No thanks."

"Sure?"

"Very."

"Well, okay. But keep in mind. A case like you I get paranoid right quick. You get weird, I'm liable to plunk you right back in the psyche bin, no questions asked. Or at least to a locked ward at the hospital. So watch yourself. There's no use pretending."

"I'm perfectly fine, sir."

"I sure hope so . . . "

ᴠ ᴠ ᴠ

Delta is diabolical in his quest for control. I must have done an incomplete job of de-bugging this place, there are still devices hidden somewhere, though I fear further dismantling because of the landlord's warning about damage. I must think of a way to maintain privacy and yet not alert the Delta control drone and cause my return to the detention zones.

ᴠ ᴠ ᴠ

I have acquired a target! I will surely survive. My energy is nearing its fullest point, close to breaking up. After so long in the drug-fog it has come back with a savage urgency, almost uncontrollable. But I won't fail the program. The target is not far from here, and fits all specifications. Hair length. Colour. Ground floor accommodation. Strong resemblance to political TV reporter. One of the better targets in long years of searching. I have been able to observe for two nights in a row and have the entry procedure and confinement process plotted. All that remains is the blade, important tool, and I saw what I wanted today in a pawn shop. Fortunately, these events, the culmination of my energy growth, pre-coagulation and decay, the location of a suitable target, have also come together with the sufficient accumulation of evil medication I have saved from Delta's ministrations. This I will trade on the street to gain the essential.

v v v

All objectives have been met and all plan systems are in place, running to schedule. The operation will take place in exactly three hundred seventy-eight minutes from now. I set the timer/wake-up function on my watch to insure strict adherence to the plan and settle down to wait the evening through. As a last preparation, I wrap the instrument in a fresh pair of my own undergarment. After this initial debut it is hoped a more suitable and poetic piece of covering will be available. Perhaps one of a pleasant colour. All these years of incarceration, I have not seen pink. I hope desperately for pink, but prepare myself for disappointment, as so often has been the case in the past. I find my mental processes wandering . . . . Energy congealing? Premature, but possible. I secure the blade and sit quietly facing the door, concentrating, holding my power self within my fleshly self, hoping for endurance to await the succour my target will bring. I am doing it. My centre coheres. I'll make it. But . . . a knock at the door! Disaster!

v v v

"How you doin' Stanley?"
"Mr. Delta!"

"That's right. In the flesh. Sorry to drop in on you unexpected and all, but you don't have a phone in this dump. And I didn't trust the guy in the cage out front to take a message. Hope you don't mind."

"No ... I ... "

"Gonna ask me in? Or should everybody on the tier here get in on our business?"

"Of course ... "

"Thanks. Nice place you got here. Not too lived in, though. Gonna unpack your suitcase eventually? Or is this strictly a temporary stop for you?"

"I've been busy. Haven't had a chance ... "

"It's two weeks. You should have settled in by now."

"Two weeks?"

"Uh huh. And you been acting funny since the first day."

"Funny."

"Yeah, funny. And that's not all. I talked to your doctors back at Regional Psychiatric. They explained to me what you'd be like if you quit taking your meds."

"Those people have very little insight, Mr. Delta, very little view to my soul. You would do well to rely on your own opinions."

"I try to do that, yeah."

"Do I appear dangerous to you? Do you think I am a menace?"

"Well, offhand, no. But the doctors said you might start acting like some kind of zombie, talking like a college professor and get delusions and things. Political paranoia, in your case. Stuff like that. Noticed anything you'd like to self-disclose?"

"Of course not."

"Well I have. Hate to break it to you, pal, but it's a good thing you got your case packed. I gotta rearrange your home address for awhile. Just over to Saint Paul's for a spell. Nothing serious."

v v v

Crisis! My energy block is corrupting! The rot steams in my throat as I stand here. I must do something. The power must be drained off or I'll decompose on the spot. The blade. The blade in the clothing in the suitcase with which Mr. Delta is so fixated.

v v v

"Atta boy. Close 'er up and let's get going. Maybe we can stop for a coffee on the way. No rush."

"I'm afraid that will be impossible, Mr. Delta."

"Told you right out you should call me Barry. I'm sure you're gonna be okay. Just a little hospital visit and you'll be up and around in no time."

"I'm sorry . . ."

"Hey. Put the gaunch *into* the suitcase, not out. You're gonna need that stuff. Here . . . "

Delta's hand is on my hand which holds the instrument. The feel of his flesh is heinous. I must disassemble him. For the good of all mankind. He is close to me and I can look in his eyes, synthetic blue, and see the machinery inside. God! I hate this life! Herded and oppressed by machines from hell. Grotesque monsters of control. His eyes sear into me, reading my thoughts, bleeding me. The energy is fading, resolving into putrid slush within my chest and abdomen, soon to rot through and spread its pitiful misused essence to the floor. My sword is dead. Delta rivets my hand to the suitcase with his evil claw.

Hospitals are the observatory/holding tanks used by the robot control creatures. The Delta machine speaks in its metallic voice: "Stay here awhile. Relax. Once you get back on the meds you can come out again." But I have no intention of killing myself with chemicals again, no intention whatsoever. I still have my blade, undetected in the disgusting entry charade of this machinery pigsty. The nurses move with android efficiency. Let them manipulate, tie me down and study me. I have been observing. I will find a way out.

v v v

"Look. I can't let you out of here until the doctors say. And they don't say."

"I am normal. It is cruel to be keeping me here among all these poor creatures when I am perfectly normal."

"You're not normal. Word is you were out on the street selling pills. Yours, no doubt. That may be normal for you for whatever reason, but it's not allowed, see. Something's up. And with you when something's up, people, women, get hurt. So no chances. No discussion. You get better, take your bug juice, or you rot here. That's that."

v v v

The monster now uses the correct language to describe his terrible actions. Rot. Decay. By some method he continues to look into my mind even when he is away. He knows what I am feeling. The devices are everywhere. In me. On me. On me! My watch! Digital mechanized horror . . .

Devices are everywhere, but they are not necessary in my case. The clever creatures have invaded me with the aid of a simple machine attached to my wrist. I dare not try to remove it for fear of an explosive. The only thing will be the instrument, my last hope. At the changing of the nurse/guard this evening I will make my move. Suitcase left foolishly under the bed. Stab it. Stab it, stab it and kill it. Destroy it where it sits, attached to my arm, evil roots cutting the skin, snaking through my body. Stab it. Stab it and kill it. Kill it . . .

4

A crook I was trying to talk back to jail got panicky and jumped through a window.

Driving to the office, the traffic was slow as ants in hot tar. When I got there the telephone messages were so thick the clerks assigned me an extra pigeon hole. Little pink overdue-report notes were all over my desk, like parking tickets on an abandoned car. To top it off there was no coffee left. A rough start to the day and not even noon.

In the hallway, John looked at me through the smoke of what I would guess was number four cigarillo of the day and chortled: "So, Barry. They won't even talk to ya without going and jumping through windows now, eh?"

"You'd think they'd have more respect," I said. "I just wanted to take him to jail."

"Funny how that happens . . . "

In my office the sun, laser-bright in the approaching noon, shone across my Dali poster, lighting up the detail of a crutch holding up a senseless portion of wall. I stared at it for a second, thinking I might be onto some extra meaning I hadn't seen before. John took a long drag on the brown stick and collapsed into one of my chairs. "Let's get out of this shithole," he said, breaking my Dali-concentration.

"I dunno, John. Gotta write this up. Book says you gotta write up a wild spectacular incident soon as it happens. Before the media get—"

"Media? Spectacular incident?" He dragged on the smoke, contemptuous. "What bullshit. None of anybody's business how a good PO does his job. Ah, god . . . for the old days."

"The old days."

"Yeah." John exhaled heavy tobacco-fog in all directions. The cloud drifted toward Dali. It looked good. "Come on," John said.

"Lunch?"

"Yeah, but later. I need your help."

"You need my help."

"Yeah."

"Like hell. It's fuck the paperwork. That's what you're really saying."

"Yeah, fuck it . . . "

"It can wait . . . "

"Wait forever, all I care . . . "

He struggled out of the chair and I got my jacket.

John's car was one of the good ones: big, old, domestic, a wide personal statement of consumerism at five klicks to the litre. John started her and slapped the gearshift into drive. "Goddamn thing barely started this morning."

"Good god in heaven! Call the garage, we gotta get this thing to hospital!"

"Shut up, smartass."

v v v

"What are we up to, anyway?"

"Wunna my boys's been drinking. Up at the Society . . . "

"Uh huh . . . "

"Gotta take him back."

"Dangerous?"

"Killed a man once but I think it was just personal. I like the guy, myself . . . "

"Good," I said. "Grudge killer. Best kind."

The Society is a half-way house on the east side of town. A huge wood-frame building, old, with a varied history of uses, whorehouse being one of them, according to John. We trudged up the tired steps, John leading the way, but after the second set he was wheezing. I took the lead. "All the way up," John said. I stopped on a landing two flights later. There were two doors. Loud snoring rumbled out from behind one of them. I looked back at John, puffing on the landing.

"Want me to do it?" I asked.

"You kidding . . . ?"

John took some breaths and marched up the last five steps, his face set. Without a word he advanced on the snore-door and pushed heavily on it with a large paw. The thin door slipped its latch and flung open, swinging against the wall and bouncing back at us. In one second we were both in the room. An Indian kid, about twenty, slept fully clothed on a bunk bed.

"C'mon, Charlie!" John's bark was loud but casual. "You're goin' to jail!"

There was no change in the tone of the snoring, though Charlie did shift slightly. His muddy cowboy boots rubbed the blankets.

"Wake up, son." John nudged Charlie on the shoulder. "Be polite. You got company."

Charlie's eyes fluttered, almost opened, then shut tighter than before. In the mass of bedclothes he clenched up, cold, as if dreaming of Antarctica, and pulled a blanket close to his chest. John wrenched the blanket away and we each took a shoulder and hoisted Charlie out of bed. Once vertical, he became marginally more alert; eyelids half raised, the snoring stopped and became a heavy wheeze.

"Aw, John, no . . . " Charlie's voice was thick. We dragged him through the door.

"It's cold out here!"

"Shouldn't be a problem, Charlie. You still got all your clothes on. But *whew!* The smell of your breath, lad! What you been drinking? Oven cleaner?"

John was right. Charlie's breathe-out could have blistered fibreglass. We stumbled down the stairs. Charlie fell back asleep.

"Where we going?" I asked, struggling.

"'Round the corner . . . "

We were a floor down from Charlie's. John pushed open a door with his foot. We dragged the kid into a small washroom. John took hold of him, swung him onto the toilet and let his head loll into the washbasin. "Works every time," John chuckled, turning the cold water on all the way.

Out in the car we dumped sodden Charlie in the back seat and took off down the street in the wrong direction. "Thought we were going to lock-up," I said, pointing. "It's that way."

"Oh, I think a little of what you might call your 'community diversion' should occur in this case." John stuck an unlit cigarillo in his maw and fumbled for a match.

"Never thought I'd hear words like that come out of your mouth. Creeping bureaucrat-itis of the brain . . . "

"Well, boy, stick around. Happens to the best of us . . . "

v v v

We drove through lunch-hour traffic, over the bridge, and took the turnoff for the Indian reservation. Charlie started making noises as we pulled up to a bungalow.

The place was in a clump of trees by a creek and aside from the rusting car bodies it was kind of pretty. So close to the city it seemed strange to be in sudden wilderness, with a calm in the air.

John got out and opened the door for Charlie. The two walked slowly to the house. From the car I saw an old woman come to the door, look at John, look at Charlie, then open the door wide and let Charlie in. She stood and spoke for a while with John.

ⱽ ⱽ ⱽ

Driving back, in the middle of the bridge, the car started acting up, coughing and backfiring, losing power just at the crest. John scowled, dragged the last on his smoke and fired the butt out the window. I tried to watch out the rear view mirror on my side to see if it rolled off the bridge deck. The car recovered slightly on the downward side, growling. Riding through town, I tried to calculate how long it would take a cigarillo butt to fall the hundred or so metres to the water.

And, if it landed on a barge or a boat, would it still be lit?

Barry Delta Knows That This Is Not A Dangerous Job.

Sure, he deals with killers, thieves and desperate characters all the time. But an overriding shred of common sense seems to govern all of them, even the dumbest ones: You don't piss in your own pocket. Most will do their damage outside the parole office.

If Barry makes a mistake with an ex-con, he knows it is probably not dangerous to him personally. It *is* dangerous to the next citizen this person sees.

Unfortunately.

5

On my fourth bit I got it all figured out, straight. Like, I read a few books, did some thinking about what a lot of guys and Mr. Delta told me and I knew I had it all worked out.

∨ ∨ ∨

It all has to do with the fact that when you screw up on a condition, see, like drinking or going out of the area or stuff like that, and don't do a crime, they only mostly put you into city lockup for a couple of weeks to cool off. No real cops around, just Sheriff's bulls who don't know from nothin'. And like I say I was thinkin' about all this on my fourth bit which was a bullshit go from one end to the other.

∨ ∨ ∨

These goddamn Chinks say I tried to rob their store! And that goddamn rat Dickey buggered off out of the country before the court date and didn't stay to tell 'em we were only trying to get some ice for the beer. Wrote me a letter from San Diego sayin' Wayne, I'm sorry but they got me up on this beef and I can't take a chance on takin' it so I took off with my ex-old lady and her biker dick-brain old man in a van to hang out down south a while. Well thanks a whole fuckin' lot! I said out loud to all the guys.

ᴠ ᴠ ᴠ

And that Delta, he says he felt sorry for me after it was all over 'cause he says he kinda believes me and all that but on the evidence I was guilty. One must not only be innocent, one must be seen to be innocent, to paraphrase, he says, always with the fuckin' quotes. Fuckin' great! Anyway, they give me a year on it and that put together with the year I had left and I ended up doing sixteen months and I got out just as the weather starts to screw up and rain like a bastard every day like a piss-wet blanket on your brain, y'know?

ᴠ ᴠ ᴠ

So Delta comes and picks me up at the joint and we go to that same depressing shitty stinking Sally Ann shelter again and I go holy shit! It's like a broken record. Always the same routine and Delta just sits there and shrugs and says change comes from within or something like that and I just get out of the car and don't say nothin' and go in.

ᴠ ᴠ ᴠ

But what he doesn't know, what that Delta in his snobby brain doesn't figure, is old Wayne is a smarter breed of cat than when he went in the last time. Oh yeah. He's been usin' the old noggin this boy and he got talking to a couple of old timers this bit who put a few ideas in his head about how to get along.

ᴠ ᴠ ᴠ

Plus I started reading this psychology book called something like *How To Yank Your Own Wires* or something like that by this bald-headed guy down in California where Dickey is and some day I'm gonna get that cheese-eating rot-face and grind him into tiny lumps of shit and feed him to a garbage compactor if I ever get my hands on the fucker again. Anyway, this book says to not sit on your ass and let things happen to you, you gotta go out and set things up to your own favour or something like that. I get thinking maybe that's what's been wrong with me all along, I let things and people fuck up on me 'cause I'm too much of a nice guy, too passive, like. All I ever want is a nice time with a couple of beers and a good-looking chick once in a while, y'know?

So for sixteen months I'm thinkin' about how I should get organized with my life and try to get on top of what's going on and stuff and about a month before I get out it all comes together one day while I'm havin' a shower. It hits me! I got it! Like a flash I figure I'm gonna use everything including the cops and Delta against themselves, right? Like, I figure I always get in the shit when I'm just hangin' around trying to have a good time. So I won't do that. I'll just work out a few things, save up some cash and go travelling like my soon to-be-dead shit-brain former buddy Dickey.

v v v

I'm so jazzed up I almost slip on the soap and went back to my house and tried to write all of it down even before I was dried off and the paper got all damp and mushy and then I threw it away anyhow because who wants everybody knowing what the plan is anyway? And besides, it's simple, I got it all in my head. So I start hanging out with a couple of the wheels who do banks, 'cause I figure it's time I started with something really good with real cash instead of robbing pop machines and walking around with my pockets ripping out with all the quarters and stuff, and I pick up a couple of serious pointers even though those so-called big guys don't like me too much. Too bad, fuckers, you seen the last of me anyhow, once I get out of this federal fuckin' joint. The most I'm ever gonna do again is a short bit in lockup and that's gonna be for a good reason!

∨ ∨ ∨

So I'm sittin' back in my Sally Ann bunk and I'm thinking careful about Plan A, the first part of my master strategy as I think they call it in the book, and pretty soon I got it figured out where I'm gonna get the clothes and the mask and all the stuff I need. The next day I go to the Goodwill and get the stuff and try it on in an alley and it fits just perfect and then I go and case the bank.

∨ ∨ ∨

The guys in the joint said it was a good idea to go back a couple of days in a row to watch for any type of special police patrols or anything and to hit the place at lunchtime because that's when it's most crowded. And the tellers are used to handing money out because the working crowd are all in there cashing their cheques. So I go and sit outside this bank on Georgia and watch but after a while I figure, hell, why not now? There's nobody around and it's now or never and to tell the truth I figure I might chicken out if I think about this too long so I duck into the front part where the money machines are and I slip the coat on and the mask and I just run past the line-up to the nearest teller and shout gimme the money!

∨ ∨ ∨

I hear the people in back of me start to get excited but the teller just looks at me with her thick coke-bottle-bottom glasses that look like they weigh five pounds and doesn't say anything. Then I say move, sister, I got a gun in here and I move my arm hard up against the side of my chest like I got something big under my coat and she pushes the glasses back up her nose and grabs a handful of cash and slides it over to me. I say All of it! really hard but not loud, kind of under my breath and it works! She gives me more cash and I grab it with both hands and stuff it in both pockets of the coat and just turn around and walk out.

v v v

Simple. Just like the guys said 'cause the tellers are all just girls and they don't want trouble and the bank just tells 'em to hand it over 'cause they don't want dead tellers on their hands. I almost forget to take the mask off, people start looking at me real goofy when I'm walking up the street so I whip it off really fast and smile like I was just fooling around or something, then I turn a corner and duck into Eaton's and take off the coat, roll it into a ball, walk across the store and go out the other way like Joe Shopper. I hear the cop cars coming from all around. I don't go by the bank even though I probably could and nobody would know me but I read once where the criminal always returns to the scene of the crime and I figure I gotta start bucking a trend here.

v v v

So I go home and count the money on my bunk when nobody's looking. Twelve-hundred bucks! I start thinking about all the things I'd like to spend it on, starting first with a better non-disgusting cleaner place to live away from all these puking rummies, but that's where the brain power comes in; I'm smarter than that this time around. I know that half this cash is hotter than chili peppers comin' out your asshole because it's what they call your bait money. The stuff is marked so you spend it anywhere within a hundred klicks, they catch you. You gotta sit on it awhile and spend it somewhere else. Bait money. Like they were fishing for crooks or something. Funny.

v v v

Well it's not funny enough to fool ol' Wayne this time around, so I wrap it up in newspaper and put it under my bunk and try to forget it's there and hang around the flop all day to make sure nobody has an interest. You can't trust anybody around a place like that but since I lost my black leather jacket in that Chinese grocery fuckup I haven't had anything worth stealing. Till now. Next day I just walk around town and don't do anything but go to the Goodwill and get another old coat. While I'm walking back I see another bank that looks good and I figure what the heck! I got the mask with me in my back pocket so I just mount up and ride on in. The same as last time, easy as hell I just walk out with a g-note or more and go back to my bunk and stash it in the local branch of Wayne Stickner Consolidated Mutual Savings Incorporated. Hah.

v v v

This is too easy I think to myself so I lay off for a day but the day after that I can't help myself so it's two more banks, one in the morning and one in the afternoon. Fuck me! Am I gonna have a good time when I get outta here! I figure I'm good for half-a-dozen more and then I start taking buses around town and doing jobs in the suburbs where it's even easier and the banks don't get robbed as much so the tellers hold more money. This is getting unreal! Inside of two weeks it's hard to sleep on my bed because of all the money lumps! I stop bothering to count the stuff and just try to lay it out evenly so it's not so lumpy, but then the hammer falls like I knew it would and it doesn't matter about the bunk.

v v v

The cops show up at the shelter and show this drawing to the social worker of the face of the guy they think is doing all the rummy robberies, they call it, or at least the newspaper starts calling it. I never take my mask off until I'm down the street but maybe somebody's seen me in an alley so without even asking I bundle up the cash I quit counting at eleven thousand bucks and hightail it outta there and go downtown and call Delta to tell him I can't stand it there anymore and can I find another place to live? He says okay but he wants to meet me downtown and say hello so I go to one of those hotels on the Mall and get a ten- dollar-a-night room with what's left of my welfare cheque and tell the guy I'll pay for a month if he'll wait 'til next week when I get another one. All the time just itchin' to lay some of my bank bread on him but keeping cool because of the bait money. Everything's fine the guy says and he's not even that interested so I stash the loot and go meet Delta. He just asks the usual questions and buys me a burger and sits and bullshits. Doesn't say a thing about the rummy robberies so I don't bring it up either, just says remember your restrictions.

v v v

Oh yeah, I says, no drinkin', no hanging around other cons, ackcetrah ackcetrah blah blah. He says right, remember what happened last time and I says I got set up by a buncha crazy Chinks who thought me an' Dickey, the fuckin' sleaze-rat, were tryin' to rob the place when all we wanted to do was get outta there. He says you wouldn't have been in such a jackpot if you'd have stayed away from drinking and your old joint-buddies. I says yeah maybe but what are you s'posed to be anyway, unsociable? All the guys I know are ex-cons. Anyway we talk like that for awhile and Delta leaves and I think to myself just wait buddy, your turn's coming pal, Plan B, you're gonna be useful yet ya snob-faced motherfucker!

66

I go back to my room and make sure my bundle's there and think to myself what next? How many more jobs 'til I get caught? What about if some cop's in there cashing his cheque? What about if there's a patrol car driving along the street just as I whip out with my mask still on? I tell myself to stop thinking, I'm gonna drive myself crazy or something. Just to put a lid on everything, show myself I'm not losing it, I whip downtown and hit another bank, actually the same one as on the first day but different teller!

I figure about five more jobs and I'll call it quits, but on the third I slip and fall on the floor going out, trip on some carpet or something. I guess if I wasn't robbing the place and was an ordinary citizen I could sue the place for damages or something but the only thing that happens to me is my mask comes off and I don't know, maybe they got a good look at me, maybe they didn't. One thing, I never look at the camera some of these places have so I'm sure they don't have a picture. Back in my room I figure this is it and I wrap up all the cash and put it into an ordinary brown paper bag, like I'm carrying my lunch. Only it's a pretty big lunch. But I don't figure anybody will be too suspicious and instead of going downstairs with my welfare cheque and paying for a month like I told the guy I just walk out on the street and find a bar that'll cash it and order a double whiskey and keep 'em comin' cause I got four hundred and eighty-five dollars to drink up and have a good time before I go to jail!

v v v

Everybody in the bar figures hey, this is great! A guy over there drinkin' like stink and buying rounds for everybody! So I go like that for all afternoon until I'm so pissed I can hardly walk and all the money's gone from these giant rounds I've been buyin' and I only got enough to get a cab and go in style to the parole office and turn myself in. So I stagger out with my paper bag and wave down a cab and pretty soon I'm sittin' in Delta's office and he's saying well? He's just looking at me and I can't help it, I says, well, that's a deep subject and laughing and laughing like it's the funniest thing in the world. He just keeps lookin' at me and after awhile I just say to him Mr. Delta, you were right, I'm just a big failure. Take me back to jail. And he turns all serious and says something like don't talk about yourself like that but I'm not listening because the booze is really starting to get to me and the room starts spinning so finally he gets his jacket and leads me out to his car.

v v v

We start driving and I think to myself good, right to city jail and a quiet cool-off for two weeks maybe and nobody will suspect I'm the Rummy Bandit. Life, I say, looking at the sky through the window of Delta's car, you're finally being good to me and I feel great. But the feeling doesn't last too long because Delta says what's that in the bag? The bag! I forgot about Plan C, or was it D? or some other letter. I was supposed to get rid of the bag in a locker at the bus station like I'd planned only the booze got to me and I forgot to tell the cab to stop and I break out sweating heavy because here I am sitting with this bag chock-full of bait money and we're heading for the city lock-up!

v v v

Oh man, what a fucking jam! I can't even think because the booze is melting my brains and I feel like they're all going to leak out my ears and make a mess in Delta's car. My fuckin' head, it's hard to think! I gotta pull myself together. I start thinkin' one last shot, Wayne boy, one last thing to figure out or you're a goner! Look, Mr. Delta, I says, could we stop at the bus station? I gotta do something. I mean, if I'm going to jail I gotta take care of some things, you know?

v v v

But Delta just looks at me with those hang-doggy eyes of his with those big pouches underneath and then I know I've had it because I suddenly gotta barf, really honk my guts out and it comes up so fast there isn't even time for Delta to stop. We're in the middle of traffic anyways so I just bend over and start spraying all over the floormat, going like hell because I drank a shitload of whiskey and I feel like I'm gonna puke my guts right out, leaning over clutching the paper bag between my legs and horkin' like crazy. I hear Delta give a groan and I guess I can understand because who wants some drunk to drop his lunch all over the floor of your car anyway?

v v v

But it wasn't so bad 'cause I haven't eaten anything and it was all whiskey anyway, probably dry up in a few hours and you'd never know it'd happened, you know? Anyway, I'm leaning over with my face to the floor heaving and thinking things like that when it comes to me that I've still gotta figure something out about this bag of moolah. I mean I'm fucked, skewered, buggered up the asshole dry if I can't come up with something, y'know? One hell of a feeling, desperate, like you got to piss and shit at the same time, only worse, because there's no easy solution, you can't just find a bathroom and make it alright. All I can see is the time I'm gonna do and the cash I'm gonna lose and I can't help thinking that my life has come to zilch, like, this is it, y'know, ralphing your guts out in your PO's car, heading to jail. What a failure! So while I'm down there barfing and sweating my insides out trying to spew and think at the same time I notice that the seats of Delta's car have enough space under them to slide something in there so I try the package and manage to get it not only under but up somewhere inside the seat so it doesn't even show there's anything under there. I push it up there really good and figure to some day get it out or steal Delta's car when the heat blows over. Then the car stops and Delta says you okay?

ᴠ ᴠ ᴠ

I say yeah but sorry about your car and Delta says forget it. I lean back in my seat and take a good breath and try to get ready to walk in the jail but then I notice we're parked outside the Sally Ann shelter. Delta goes look Wayne, you're a goofball, there's no denying that, but I feel you deserve something for that Chinese grocery thing. So I'm giving you a break and you can sleep it off in here, he says. Aw damn, I says, I can't stand it no more and he says you'll feel better in the morning, Wayne and before I can do anything he's out of the car and around to my side and got me by the arm and pulling me into the flophouse.

They dump me on one of the detox bunks and leave me there and I pass out before I can think up a way to get the money back or what the hell to do next anyway. In the middle of the night I wake up still drunk but clear enough to know I gotta get outta there because the town is really hot for me now and I don't want the cops coming back around and asking questions like before because you never know when those guys are gonna get lucky. So I roll off my bed and get the hell outside into the fresh air and go sleep the rest of the night with the rummies under the Georgia viaduct where you can almost get warm if the wind isn't blowing too hard. In the morning I walk around for a while and then phone Delta and say to him look, I think I better go back to jail, I mean, I can't make it out here.

But he says nonsense, you're perfectly capable of almost anything if you put your mind to it. Do you want a job? I know of a job. And I yell at him no, I don't want a job! I'm a fuckin' bum don't you know that? I don't wanna work so put me in jail where

I belong but he just says don't be silly and says he's busy and just hangs up.

v v v

What the hell am I gonna do! The streets are hot for me, I just gotta lay low in some city cell with a bunch of drunks if I'm gonna have any chance of waiting for the heat to die down. I got no money, I'm hungry as hell, I got no place to stay. And I even lost my bank profits. Even though I can't spend it it would sure be nice to have it just to hold onto. Fuckin' eh, I'm thinking to myself, walking around town, what's goin' on, anyway? One minute you're sittin' on top of the world, next thing you know you get kicked in the nuts by fate. What the hell is the use of goin' on anyway?

v v v

I start swearing to myself, walking around town, around and around and finally I just sit on a bus-stop bench and almost start crying right there like a baby and then I sit up and say watch it, Wayne, this is the way you start thinking when you screw up all the time so just cut it out. Remember what that guy in that book said. Don't let things get you down so easy. Think of something. And I'm thinking away when this guy sits down beside me and says hi Wayne and I look up and it's that Davey Patterson who did time the same place as me one time a couple of years ago and I kind of say hi to the guy but I'm not too glad to see him because we never got along anyway. Small-time drug dealer stolen goods kind of guy thinks he's real hot shit, got this old lady who's this expensive hooker but both of 'em are dead now I hear and good riddance but he turns to me and says wanna talk with ya, come on. And I says no, Dave, I'm waitin' for a bus, we talk right here. And he says watch yourself asshole or I'll stick you right here. I been watching you, he says, you're the Rummy Bandit and you're gonna cut me in or take a lickin' right here. I says you're fulla shit Patterson and get off my cloud and I get up to go but the guy swings a blade at me and cuts me down the back. Right through my shirt.

I go down on the sidewalk and flip over and start thrashing and yelling and a lot of people start staring and hanging around. Patterson takes another swipe at me but only sticks my boot and then he buggers off down the street but there's a police car pulled up on the curb and he damn near runs right into it still with the knife out in his hand. They start going after him and I get up and boot it into an alley and into the back of a parkade and hide between a couple of cars for a while until the commotion dies down.

v v v

I figure it's tits up for me now even if Patterson doesn't cop to the cops about what I been doing which he probably won't but it means a lot of people are gonna be after me and my life's not worth a plugged shit if they catch me around here. I figure I gotta get out of town so I start walking even though my back hurts like hell from that knife cut but it's not bleeding and by night I'm somewhere out in the 'burbs someplace and hungrier'n fuckin' hell.

I think I'm gonna puke my guts out again even though I haven't even got anything to upchuck. I mean it's really gross this whole situation and I don't even want to walk anymore, I just want the whole thing to be over. I try to sleep in this culvert but it's no good, it's too wet and there's not many places to curl up, you know, the 'burbs are all like that, everybody with a cut lawn and neat fences and all that. Everybody looks home so there's no sense trying to break in anywhere. And I'm so hungry I think I could eat my own hand, it's that bad, things are getting desperate. I wish I was back in town even if it is hot for me there.

Finally I get so cold and hungry I go to one of those all-night stores with the clerk who wears one of those uniforms with the store colours on it and there's a sign that says less than twenty dollars in till after ten p.m. I go in and wander around the back trying to get warm and then when there's nobody else in the store I go up to the guy at the counter, he's a pimply kid about nineteen and say, how about a hotdog? and I point to those ones they have wrapped up behind the glass that they throw in the microwave for about thirty seconds.

The kid says you mean you want to buy one? I says yeah, sure and the kid says where's your money? and I say hold your horses, that's not all the stuff I want. So I turn around and go get all kinds of stuff, potato chips, bottles of pop, chocolate bars, all the things I been dreaming about eating for the last twelve hours and go back to the counter with them. The kid's got the hotdog out but he holds it back and says I'll heat it up but you gotta pay for it first, and I says go ahead and fumbles with my pockets. I look up and he's still just standing there with the hotdog in his hand. I figure it's now or never, I gotta have something to eat or I'm just gonna die on the spot. I whip the hotdog out of his hand and grab some chips and dash for the door.

v v v

When I get to the door I gotta whip the hotdog from one hand to my chip hand to grab the door handle and while I'm doing that the kid comes up to me and says hold it. Kid moved fast, must have jumped the counter or something. I turn around and he's got a two-by-four ready to bean me if I move one inch. Musta had it under the counter. He's wound up like a baseball player ready to hit a homer with my head so I don't move but I just say come on kid, gimme a break. He stands there with the two-by-four ready and says real tough forget it, drop the stuff and leave and don't come back or I'll call the cops.

v v v

I think to myself why does this always happen to me? Why does there always have to be someone there who says no, Wayne, you can't have that. You can't have anything, your name is Wayne, get out of here you're not welcome, Wayne. Fuck.

v v v

The guy is standing there and I can tell from his eyes he'd like to hit me. Imagine that, what did I ever do to this guy? I says to him, I says, gee, you don't know how hungry I am. He says right back, I don't care. He don't care. He don't fuckin' care. Okay. If he doesn't care well fuck neither do I. Fuck, I don't care. What does he know about me? He doesn't know what's happened to me. He don't care. Okay, buddy, you don't care, well neither do I and I go down and drive my head into his stomach before he has time to do anything.

It's pretty hard to hit yourself in the gut with a club which is what he would have had to do to get me once I lunged at him. He went backwards and stumbled up against a magazine rack and he and me and it went crashing to the floor. I got the stick of wood out of his hands right away, he tried holding on but it was no use and I hit him right away, in the head, on the neck, on the back, wherever I could get a clear shot, I just hit him and hit him.

v v v

You don't care, huh? Did you get cut with a knife today? Huh? Did you lose all your money in somebody's car and not know if you're ever going to get it back? Did you spend all your welfare? I hit him and hit him. Hit and hit and hit until I felt better and I started not even caring about being hungry or without a place to stay for the night. I didn't care about jail or the cops or anything like that. I just hit and hit. Then the two-by-four was out of my hands and I looked around and a guy, looked like a cab driver with a little hat and a change belt, was standing there with it in his hands. I just laughed and went over and sat in a corner until the cops got there and took me away.

v v v

They took me away and booked me on attempted murder right there even before they called Delta to get my supervision lifted. They took me downtown and told me to clean the blood off my hands, they were going to put me in a line-up for the Rummy Robberies. After the line-up a detective got me in a room and said I was lucky because nobody could identify me but it didn't matter because it looked like I was going away for a long time anyway. He asked me why a guy like Davey Patterson would take a swipe at me but I just dummied up and let him do all the talking.

v v v

Delta finally showed up but didn't talk to me at first, just looked through the bars and shook his head. So much for Plan C, or B, or whatever it was. D, F, G and Z. Whatever. But then he turned around all of a sudden and they let him in the cell and locked us up together and he sat down, looking at me. He said why'd you do the kid like that?

But I'm not that dumb so I didn't flap about it. They get you to talk about one beef so's you'll crack open on another. I know their tricks.

v v v

So he just sits there looking at me almost crazy and says who do you think you are? Huh, I say. Who do you think you are and who do you think he is? Huh? You think that kid doesn't think a lot like you? You think you don't come from the same side of the tracks? How do you know?

Huh? I says to him, but he doesn't shut up, not Delta, you know, the man talks like some kind of machine when he gets going, it's awful. He says you don't think maybe there's maybe just two paycheques difference between you and him? He stares at me, crazy. I think I'm gonna get a lickin' the way he stares at me. You went outside, he yells, you went outside and beat on a civilian. He keeps on, you went outside, he says, bad enough you beat on each other but you broke the rules, you went outside. Delta keeps raving, he kicked the bars and shook his head so much I figured it was going to fall off.

v v v

The kid didn't die so they made me on an assault causing bodily harm. They were gonna go with attempt murder but I offered to cop to it and my lawyer got a deal so they reduced it. Still got ten years on it though. Fuck. Anyway, I almost had things on the go out there this time, fuckin' eh. I figure, last time it took me sixteen months to come up with a plan, this time I got ten odd years to work on it, so hey I'm trying to look on the bright side. No telling what I can dream up. I'm working on it up here in my little brain, for sure, old Wayne isn't gonna waste all his time. Besides, it's better than just sittin' here, wondering what Delta's gonna do.

Barry Delta Knows That He Is Sole, Alone, In Any Matter He Cares About, And Dependant On No-one But His Ever-doubting Self.

These dead people under the blotter, they didn't figure things out. They never defined themselves in any context. Barry knows this because he cajoled enough, talked himself dry in the head enough times to realize it was foolish to try to get someone to look at themselves and really see. Especially not in the experiential world they were occupying. There's only so much faith you can have in things you can't see, feel, touch, eat, kill or fuck. Only so much. For some, hardly any at all.

6

One day when Barry Delta thought he was being so good, so good—Janice walked out on him. It started ten days before with a click, the sound of her toothbrush going into the little stand by the sink as Barry entered the bathroom. The click was a more solid sound than usual, harsher than what he was used to. He was surprised he could be so sensitive to certain things. Then he foggily connected her force in plunking down the toothbrush to the possibility she might be bothered by something. He rubbed his head, and leaned against the wall.

"Something wrong?" he asked her.

"Two years," said Janice, leaning close to the mirror, inspecting her eyelids. "I have to be honest. It's bugging me." She did not look at him.

"Oh . . ."

Nothing else came to his mind. He rubbed his head some more, hopeful, and sleep-stumbled out of the bathroom to the kitchen to get coffee. He tried to think clearly. No luck.

But it didn't matter, at least not that first day. They left it at that: the hard clink of a toothbrush. There was no sense starting on a bedrock issue thirty-five minutes before worktime. Not for something Barry knew would take a lot of time and care, much more than he was able to give right then. Probably more than he was ever able to give.

Able or willing? He tried not to upset himself, thinking.

At the office, before he could think about anything, Barry got a call from Patricia, the hooker girlfriend of one of his favourite parolees. "Hi, Pat," he said. "Look, could you hold on a sec. I just walked in. I need some coffee."

"They picked him up yesterday," said Pat, in a whiskey-drinker's rasp. The woman was young, but her voice was fifty.

"They did, huh. Any idea what for?"

"You don't know?"

"I just got in. Gimme a break."

The sandpaper voice began to talk. Barry's mind gripped the voice and brought up the face on his thought screen. A beautiful face, though a little hard; not yet ruined by sadness. "Meet me for lunch," the voice said.

"Uh . . . Can't today. Or tomorrow either. Day after."

"Is that soon enough?"

"He's not going anywhere."

"Fine."

When she hung up Barry regretted not having listened. To either Janice or Patricia. What kind of trouble was Davey Patterson in now? What kind of trouble was *he* in?

Despite the work at hand, he decided to devote some thinking to Janice. Did he love this woman? For two years she'd watched him go to work and come home and fitted so well into his life. What was going on, here?

v v v

Later in the day when his focus had changed several times and he'd had four cups of coffee Barry started chasing the Davey Patterson story.

He called the police: "Understand you've got one of mine. A Patterson?"

"Right."

"What have you got?"

"Tried to tickle one of his old cell mates with a little knife. Guy named Wayne Stickner."

"Oh hell, he's mine too."

"What kinda place you running there, Delta? Can't you keep these guys away from one another?"

"This is puzzling. There's no connection between them. They've never had anything to do with each other. They're two completely different kinds of crook. Generally avoid each other like work. Something must be up."

"You're telling *me*?"

v v v

Work kept Barry on the job until almost midnight. Things were happening. Wayne Stickner was brought in late in the evening for a bloody convenience-store robbery. Davey was put into cells at the city lock-up, anxiously awaiting the judge and jury of Barry Delta to come and pass judgement.

When he got home, Janice wanted to talk.

"I'm sorry for laying that strange mood on you. Especially with no warning. It was just another one of the things that are going wrong."

"It's okay . . . "

Barry stopped short. Janice's eyes showed quick anger.

"How can you say that? It's obvious that I'm hurting. How can you say it's okay?"

"I know. I can't. You're right. I'm sorry. I'm tired. Can we talk tomorrow?"

Janice turned away, fighting a tear in her eye. Barry shucked off his jacket and slumped into a chair.

Janice made Barry's breakfast on the morning of the third day and he grabbed her as she placed the bowl of seven grain cereal on the kitchen table. He grabbed her, feeling like she was the major love of his life, and sat her on his knee.

"Babe . . . " He nuzzle-spoke into her ear.

She was languid in non-response. Barry kept nuzzling anyway. Finally she said: "Let's go out tonight."

Barry disengaged. "Okay. Where?"

"I don't know. To eat . . . "

"Sure."

Barry tried to ignore the sticky silence. They'd been talking, he thought, talking recently about their problems. At least, they were talking about talking about their problems. Without thinking too heavily, he thought, things were okay.

Davey Patterson was a fine-looking man, even in prison greens, and no kid. In fact he was two years Barry's senior. Their interviews sometimes impressed Barry as a little absurd; younger brother scolding older brother. So far, absurd or not, nothing had worked.

The gate opened, Barry watched Patterson walk through and follow the pointing finger of the guard. Davey entered the cramped cubicle, sat down, and rested his arms on the flimsy table. Barry met his eyes with an impassive stare. "So," he said, "back in."

"A visit. Not permanent."

"Let me be the judge of that. What were you thumping Wayne Stickner for?"

"You know him?"

"Somewhat."

"Well, I didn't touch the fuckin' little rat."

"Rat? Hold on. Wayne is stupid, yes. But no rat."

"It's complicated."

"I've got time."

"Naw . . . "

"Favour for somebody? No names just nod yes or shake no."

81

"Doesn't matter."

"What? The favour, or the fact you're in again when everything was going sort of okay?"

They stared, silent for a moment. Barry felt a heat coming to his face. Davey avoided Barry's gaze.

Barry said: "Wayne Stickner is nothing but a profoundly dumb slob who can't even rob a corner grocery store. What the hell were you doing laying down law to a small-timer like that?"

Davey just looked at Delta and said nothing. In the code of prison this was required of him. Barry knew this as well as anybody but was duty-bound to chase that rabbit anyway.

"Pat called," Barry said. "I'm seeing her for lunch."

"Good. Tell her to relax."

"That's for you to tell her."

"Can't."

"Why not? Can't she visit?"

"Aw . . . Don't want her coming to places like this," Davey said, glancing aside.

P atricia wasn't very old, maybe twenty-seven; an experienced woman with no pretensions, a uniqueness of face and eye, and a luxury of mouth and body that made it easy to think of why uncomplicated, busy men might readily hand over one thousand dollars for a weekend of her company.

Barry was meeting her in a restaurant, one of the open-air trend-spots on Robson where everybody keeps their sunglasses on. He sat at a table sipping mineral water and waited, then saw her get out of a taxi. He was mildly shocked to see the age her face betrayed from the across-the-street distance. Since last he'd seen her, maybe two months, things were different. No wrinkles from here, but the sunken eyes of trouble. Walking toward him, looking down to replace bills in a clutch purse, Barry watched the face until the shortened range covered the sad mask and the make-up worked its perfection again.

She smiled, waved, moved like a cougar through the tables and sat down.

v v v

"They're charging him with possession of a weapon."

"That little knife?"

"So you know he was walking around with a blade. So you're as dumb as he is. Why?"

"It's just a letter opener. You never know when you'll get mail."

"Hardy har . . . "

"Really, Barry, you're such a nice guy. And kind of good looking. Why don't we have a party sometime?"

"No thanks . . . . Don't change the subject."

"Oh, don't be so stuffy."

"I can't afford it."

"Don't worry about that. On the house. Just you and me. You're really overdue, you know. Most men wouldn't have known me as long as you, seen me in my house, bought me lunch, babysat my sweetie, and not have done something about it by now."

"I know it would be nice. Don't worry. But don't tempt me with that kind of stuff, Pat, give me a break. Why was he carrying a knife and out looking to puncture a little guy like Wayne Stickner?"

"Who?"

"Exactly. That's what's so stupid. If Davey's taking little contracts like I kind of now think he might have been, well, that pickles it for me. I mean, we're all grownups here, we shouldn't try to kid ourselves. This isn't any kind of big league. What is he . . . bored? Does it bug him with you out working, bringing home the bacon and eggs and him just lying around watching daytime TV?"

Barry was surprised how hard the makeup had to work to mask Patricia's feelings. She looked down, face hardening, and pulled a cigarette out of the little purse. There was no speaking until smoke passed her nostrils, the lingering greyness giving suggestion of what this woman would look like in years to come.

"Look, Barry. A man's in jail who wants to come out to his woman. You can understand that. I'm sure you've got a girlfriend. A guy like you." She looked at him, changed, became honey-eyed again. "Come on and be a sweetie . . . ."

Barry tried to assess the possible meanings in her troubled eyes, weighing the tone her voice had taken. "You can't help him with that kind of stuff," he said. "I'm immune, sort of."

"Well how . . . ?"

"Talk to him. He's gotta crack to me. I can't do anything otherwise. Talk to him and then talk to me and I'll go talk to him and maybe we can do something."

"Promise?"

"Of course." Barry smiled. "Anything for you, Pat."

"There you go again, being nice. And you won't let me do anything for you."

"I told you. Don't tempt me . . . "

The rest of lunch passed sociably. When they got up to go, she took a tweed fistful of his sleeve and leaned up to give a kiss on the cheek and said: "You're a peach." Then he went his way and she went to her afternoon.

Janice phoned Barry at the office: "We have to talk."

He almost reflexed: "What about?" but wisely caught himself. Eight years of street work had given him something besides grey hair at the temples. Instead, he said: "I know. Let's have lunch."

"No. I mean we need help. Counselling."

"Counselling."

"Yes. I got a referral to someone. There's an opening this afternoon."

"This afternoon."

"Yes. Can you do it?"

She was asking a lot, but made it sound like only: Can you rearrange your day? To Barry the question was: Do you want to work at us or not? Do you believe in talking? Do you think we can make it? Can you only problem-solve with other people and not yourself? Are you worth having a relationship with anyway?

"Sure," he said quickly.

"It's for two-thirty. Is that okay?"

"Yes."

They met in the waiting room and, uncomfortable, facing the unknown, held hands and spoke in low voices. The counsellor was a serious-faced man with a lot of gray hair. Smart enough looking, Barry thought, but strangely awkward, aloof; giving the strange impression of never having been in a relationship himself. Barry hoped to be mistaken.

The counsellor took them to a pleasant, windowed office and asked a few light questions to get the session going. After a few minutes he turned to Janice and said: "You're troubled. What might be the problem?"

"Barry has been very honest with me. He can only go so far in a relationship. I want more. I feel so terrible to ask for more but I need more."

Janice began to cry. The counsellor gave her a tissue and let her weep for a moment. He turned to Barry. "What do you feel to see Janice cry?"

"I feel sorry." It was hard to push the words out. "I feel very much distressed but I guess if that's what she has to do then I guess it's best to let her just cry."

Barry tried and failed to say all of his words eye to eye with the counsellor. The windows offered views of a children's park and the far street. He gazed outside. The counsellor leaned slightly forward in his chair. "Just cry," he echoed.

"Yes," Barry said, watching a truck go down the street. "Just cry."

The truck took a corner and slowly rumbled out of sight. Barry watched its exhaust fumes roil in the air and fade. He was conscious of Janice's sobs, and the otherwise silent room. He was aware of the counsellor. He thought to himself about the disappeared truck, about Janice, about Davey Patterson and Pat. He kept on thinking. He thought about what it would be like to make love to Pat. He knew he would never share his whole life, his other lives, with any one person at any one time.

Barry kept staring down the street. The truck fumes were completely gone.

On the fifth day after the toothbrush went clanging down into its holder in Barry and Janice's bathroom, Barry again walked into the barred, grungy environment of the city jail. Davey Patterson was brought down and without saying hello, took a seat in the interview room.

Barry did not say hello either, but got right to the point: "Pat been in?"

"Yeah."

"Well .. ?"

"Okay. I got tired of lying around."

"Right. Go on."

"So, I got some work."

"Through the classified ad section of the newspaper."

"Come on."

"I can't be hanging around here all day."

"Okay."

"Okay."

"So that's it. That's all there is."

"No."

"Aw, come on. You want names or something?"

"Of course not. Just tell me why you were crazy enough to take something like this when things are going great for eight solid months. I mean, you got a good old lady, you got school, you're

86

looking at nine more if you screw up plus whatever they give you on any new beef. Tell me about it. You don't have to name names."

"A couple of guys get mad at this one guy for doing some things they told him about so they want somebody to scare this guy so he goes away. Simple."

"What could be so sizzling hot that they'd want a guy like Wayne to sit up and listen? I mean, I'm missing something here."

"Oh yeah? Well put your ear to the ground and ask some people back at the joint. The guy's back in now . . . "

"I know . . . "

"That's not all of it. Look, it doesn't have to do with a lot of logic, get it? It's a pride thing. You got some big fucking bruisers doing time out at that place. Some of 'em got cash from before and they buy what they want. Somebody pisses them off, somebody says something they shouldn't say or sits in the wrong chair in the TV room or anything like that, they get their feelings hurt. They want a guy to shut up, they pay to have somebody do the job. You know all this. Why the fuck am I telling you all about this?"

"Because you want to get out. And you won't get out unless you tell me what you were doing and why and what you're going to do different next time."

"My lawyer was in here. He says the knife thing is no sweat 'cause it's a small one and I never went down for a weapons beef before. He figures a fine. Maybe a day in jail or something."

"Good for you but that still doesn't solve our immediate problem. Should I cancel your suspension and take a chance on you going out and playing gangster again on some poor defenseless lower class crook or should I hand the whole thing over to the parole board like I feel like doing and let you take your chances on a nine year remainder? Let's see, you go down right now they'd never give you another parole so you'd do two thirds that's six out of nine and be out just about in time for your big four-oh birthday party. Don't worry, I don't expect an invite . . . "

"Jee-zuz, Barry . . . "

"Now don't get religion on me. It's been tried before. Won't work."

"Hmmm . . ."

"Besides, you don't need religion. I checked with your instructors at the correspondence school, they say you were doing great."

"Oh yeah?"

"Yup. Figure you would've passed everything if you'd stayed. Couple of 'em said they'd take you back and give you credit for this semester if you went right to it. Would you do that?"

"You asking me just for fun or what? I mean, what does it matter, right?"

"It might matter, Davey, if you'd get off your soft sorry ass and fight for yourself for a change. You want to think life has done this to you, these wonderful surroundings, all the sweet things you've done in your time. But it's you, friend, just you. You are the problem here. Just as it's you who will handle this situation and get you out of it if you get out at all. You hearing me?"

"Yeah."

"You want to get out?"

"Yeah."

"Okay, fine. You'll be ridden like you've never been rode before. I want to hear from you every day. I even want to see your essays and exam papers. I don't want to hear any shit. Any shit I hear, you could find yourself back here real fast and I won't even come to say goodbye. Okay?"

"Yeah."

"Good. You're a lot of work, Davey, but you got a nice girlfriend."

They said hello, cooked dinner together, spoke of work that day and tomorrow, sat eating and sipping wine and then finally Barry remembered the session and brought the subject up, worried he'd left it too long.

"I felt better afterward," Janice said.

"I felt awful," said Barry. "It made me uncomfortable . . . "

"You don't like seeing me cry?" Her voice had a harder edge than it should have.

"No, no . . . I didn't like that guy. I don't think he's connected, you know? I don't know. I'm glad you feel better."

"I said I felt better after the session. Crying sort of got it all out. Temporarily. There's still problems."

"Yeah, I know . . . "

But he didn't know. His mind started wandering again. Did he want it to? He daydreamed. The sound of her voice was doing that to him lately. She stopped. He hadn't been listening.

She looked at him with clear, examining eyes. She'd been speaking and he hadn't been listening.

"Huh?" he said.

"Sometimes I almost think there's someone else. The way you act. I know you like me. But you don't seem to want this relationship anymore."

"I love you," he said, a fearing, dread-sickness fouling his stomach. "Don't be silly." The foulness rose to his chest.

"I know there's no one else," she said. "That almost makes it worse."

"Of course there's no one else," he said, relieved that it was the truth.

Janice turned to her food, started to speak, did not, ate a little and looked at him. Her expression was tender. He smiled, knowing there would be no more relationship talk that night.

Thank god that's settled, he thought. But the sick feeling did not fade quickly.

Upon release, Davey Patterson proceeded directly home, gathered his school books and hightailed it to a late afternoon class. He managed to talk to three professors and had things pretty well patched up by the time he phoned Barry Delta.

"It's just like you said. Everything's cool."

"You expected less?" Barry smiled, putting down the phone. Another happy customer. He'd spoken to a secretary friend of his at the prosecutors office who let him in on the fact that the police had not even submitted the knife business for legal action, maybe hoping instead to use the threat of a weapons charge to turn Davey Patterson some time in the future. Fat chance. They should have known they were dealing with a better criminal than that, recent lapses aside. Davey had been one of the best drug traffickers in the city, and only got caught because of a weakness for women with a weakness for his product. That's where things with Pat were different. From all appearances the lady was not a drug-pig, like many of the women working the street. Maybe that's why she had a higher class of business, and didn't have to stand around on street corners. Whatever the case, letting Davey go was saving the taxpayers a shitload of money, made a lot of sense, might result in the eventual complete salvage of a human being and just plain made Barry feel good.

v v v

Unfortunately for all concerned, there was one person still upset and unhappy with the arrangements. Wayne Stickner stalked the prison yard. He watched Davey Patterson gain his release, sauntering through the prison gates on the way, Wayne knew, to his girlfriend's arms.

Wayne thought hard, trying to be positive, and a plan came to him. He sought out two inmates he slightly knew and huddled with them in the yard. He spoke of his plan.

"Yeah, well," said the first one, "you ain't got the dough, so shut it."

"Fuck you I ain't. You don't know nothin'. You don't know who's talkin' to ya right now."

"What's this shit?" said the other man.

"I says you know anybody gettin' out?" persisted Wayne.

90

"When?"

"Now."

"Me. Who cares?"

Wayne pulled a crumpled news clipping from his pocket. It was a picture of himself as the Rummie Bandit.

"Okay, this is me and me is this. You wanna make some?"

"After I get my piece 'tail, might," said the first man.

"Come through on this you get the cash and the tail, all in one cute deal. But you listen."

"Okay, I listen."

"What about you?" Wayne asked the second prisoner.

"I'm gone next week."

"Okay. You guys pull this I know where you get lotsa money."

On his second day out Davey answered the door to two somber-faced men. In the instant that it took, he decided that he had once known one of them in a long ago, couple-of-month-long bit he'd done in a forestry camp for stealing a car. The other one he did not know. The two, Davey could see, had been sent. The why was immaterial. It was enough that they had been sent. No words were spoken. The one Davey slightly knew moved his hand inside his jacket pocket.

Patricia was home at the time. Davey hoped, as he reflexively slammed the door back shut, that she was out of her long shower and had something on. There was running to do.

In Davey's life there had been much pain. His father was a physical abuser, his mother drew blood where it did not show. Davey was no stranger to hurt, the giving and receiving. He knew how to fight. He knew he could handle these guys if he could get a handle on the situation, and the only bug was having Pat flouncing around with her beautiful tits bared and walking in on this jam-up without knowing.

Davey's force, leaning into the door, was good. Slamming closed, it struck one guy in the foot and did damage. He pushed the door all the way to the end and latched it, twisting the lock, knowing the split second it took may earn him only a split second more in turn for the boys to come through.

"Pat!" He knew he may only get one word out, it had to express a lot. She had to understand and act, fast. He could not help her move, but only give her a little time to do so. The word was barely out when the door splintered loudly.

The sound of rending wood was all the backup illustration Patricia needed to the shout of her name from the front door. It had sounded urgent enough, but through the space of down the hall, through the closed door and through the heavy steamed air of the bathroom, it could have been a cough, it could have been a curse. The splitting door made it a story, one she was not particularly strange to. She had towelled off, ready to go out and get her clothes on. She pulled on panties, all she had, and wrapped the biggest towel around her and cracked the door for a look.

Two men and Davey battled in the hall for control of the day. The two had knives, though one stood back, leaning against the wall and followed the action off-kilter, favouring a tender foot. The other heavily tried to grasp Davey with his free hand, jab with the other. Davey struggled with a jagged piece of the wooden door.

Patricia did not have to think about her next move. In fact, the drill had once been discussed by her and Davey as casually as any household might devise their fire drill. She sprinted through the living room, slid open the glass door and bounded for the sun deck railing, holding her towel. The plan was to slip onto the outside and sidestep over to the other apartment, the decks being separated by a thick wooden divider. This was not a particularly dangerous thing to do as the apartment was only on the second floor, but once out, clinging by hands behind her back, Patricia was unnerved by the hard look of the ground below. She was over the parking lot, asphalt, and there was a nasty-looking three-foot retaining wall sticking up at her for extra trouble should she fall.

Inside the apartment the sounds of war escalated. There was a shocking slam against the wall that made Patricia's railing shudder. The towel dropped from around her, wrapped in a clingy wide ribbon about her legs and left her breasts cooling in the fresh air. Despite this she was doing fine. Only three feet to go before she could swing around and get a leg up in neutral territory.

Davey had the door-shard swinging. The active one backed away, thinking. Davey drove a sharp end into the leaning one's chest, feeling some yield. The man screamed.

Patricia did not know whose scream it was, but she tensed in reaction and lost her backward grip on the railing and came scratching and teetering loose, going to space. If she attempted to control her descent, to try to land on her feet and only suffer broken ankles and maybe chipped teeth, the railing-fouled towel ruined all that. As she fell, just enough drag yanked her feet and set her in a swan-dive plunge, an adrenaline panic-surge causing her to pull hands to face and gather her knees, a facedown, kneeling figure. She quivered, in the frozen moment, recalling revulsion and the boredom of school, the smell of her mother's toilet water and her step daddy's hand up her leg. Her forehead struck the retaining wall and the last three feet of the journey did not matter.

Back in the apartment, Davey was getting proud of himself. He'd forced the two to regroup back in the hallway, one of them seriously harmed, and had him a weapon in the door part that served his purpose with unexpected efficiency. He leaned against the wall, tried to get his breath, and listened for the two inept, heavy-breathing assassins. It occurred to him that the best defence in a situation like this was an offence and without any more thought ran into the hallway, slashing with his club. He connected twice, doing little harm, but the boys on the payroll retreated for the last time, running down the hall injured and staggering, Davey close after them. Almost hoping one of them would turn, stand and try to fight.

They clattered down the stairwell out of sight and Davey paused for a moment, collecting his breath, making sure they were gone, before going back to the apartment to see how Pat made out.

v v v

"Is this Delta? Parole service?"

"Yes."

"Detectives. We got one of yours."

"Which one?"

"Patterson."

"Again? I just arranged for him to get out."

"We noticed that. Nice going. Just chucked his prosty-whore girlfriend off the sundeck of their happy home. Real rehab work you got going there. Punched her up pretty bad. She won't live."

"Shit."

"Thought you'd say something like that. Anyways, he's sitting in lock-up. We don't have witnesses yet but the place looks beat up pretty bad. Guess he was giving her the weekly rough-up so she'd do a better job on the street. All over now, though. You can write this one off."

"There's something wrong."

"You're telling *me!*"

Barry went to see Patricia in the hospital. She was unbelievably messed up, and died the next day. Twenty-four hours later, Davey Patterson was found dead in his cell of a drug overdose. Intentional or otherwise, no one cared enough to work on a theory either way.

Barry was hard at paperwork the afternoon of their second appointment with the counsellor and he worked right through and didn't even think about it.

John looked into Barry's office late in the afternoon and whistled. "Quitting time, boy. Git home to that woman of yours, she's gonna be pissed off."

"She'll understand, John. I gotta finish this. I mean, I'm looking like an ass on this one. Not that I care, but the real story has to come out somehow ... "

"Real story?" John said, lighting the last work-time cigarillo of the day. "Who are you? Sam Spade? How the hell are you ever gonna get the real story?"

Barry stared for a moment at nothing. Then back at the thicket of forms and paper on his desk. "Yeah," he said. "I guess you're right."

John left. Barry stayed awhile longer, staring at the paper and then tried again to write the *real* story. It was the tenth day since the toothbrush dropped, Barry did not know that *the* story was still going on.

v v v

Janice waited at the counsellor's office until half an hour past the appointed time and then, at the invitation of the counsellor, went in herself for a short session. For some time, she told him, things had been foggy between she and Barry. She'd had trouble making up her mind about things. She couldn't think or see clearly. As she spoke, however, like sun-dried clouds on a summer day, the fog began to clear. She spoke more, and then knew almost what to do. She felt proud that she did not cry.

v v v

It was almost midnight when he got home. Janice had packed most of her stuff. It sat in the middle of the hall in boxes. All of her clothes were gone. There was no note. He thought, painfully and hard, sitting on a box in the hall, about the truth. The real story. He felt afraid and knew that the truth of it was he hadn't seen it

95

coming, the fact of her leaving, just as he hadn't seen the leaping of a prostitute from an apartment balcony or the dud ending of her misguided outlaw hero. These things had just happened, and it wasn't necessarily Barry Delta to stay with any woman, and it wasn't so bad for the world to lose another dumb hooker and her goofy boyfriend. It felt like something he'd feel sorry for and hurt over and even cry about in a couple or three years from now.

7

When you were a boy your father taught you an all-purpose slip-knot.

You learned it and used it well all the rest of your life. But when you were a little boy you boobed on it once, learning that first time, and your father clipped you on the ear. You didn't cry, you'd learned enough by then not to. When you grew up you smuggled drugs with three other guys, driving the truck across the border like a trooper. When you were caught you protected your friends and honourably went away for a longer time than would have been fair, had your three compadres shared the misfortune. When you got out you took your parole officer to the farm to see what you could really do and when you didn't close the tailgate of the truck in just such a way your father clipped you on the ear, you, a man of twenty-seven. Mr. Delta watched, trying not to show, wanting to look away. He saw what the problem might be.

ᴠ ᴠ ᴠ

When Delta sat down and talked with you in your little apartment with your week's supply of congealed campfire stew on the stove and reminisced about your crimes he said:

"Steve, there was a time in this country when a guy like you could have really made it. I mean, the kind of balls you show, you would have been good in a war or something."

But you cocked your head and made like you didn't understand.

And all the while the fly was buzzing in your ear. You looked good, red-haired and square-jawed in the mirror, even Delta said so and you knew he wasn't a fag. You ran, you swam, did push-ups, sit-ups, pull-ups, but you planned hold-ups. You had guns, and three more accomplices. You stole money and diamonds. You spoke to Mr. Delta of your midnight-to-morning job as doorman at an after-hours club. You said:

"Lotsa niggers. Fuck, you should see the guns that get flashed. All the niggers got guns."

But Delta wasn't listening. He said: "Blacks, Steve, Blacks. Nobody's a 'nigger' anymore ... "

ᴠ ᴠ ᴠ

And one day you and your friends held up the third jewelry store in a month, and someone was wise and pushed an alarm. And while you were smashing and grabbing someone outside yelled: "You in there! Police! Quit! Throw out your guns and walk out!"

One of you wanted to quit. One of you wanted to shoot. One of you wanted to hold hostages and threaten. You thought of the back door. They went out the front, fought, shooting, and ran in all directions and got away. You found the alley and no-one in it so you ran down, ripping your mask, shedding your overcoat until only your gun remained. You found a door that was locked with a shootable lock. You almost shot, but thought, banged on the door, not to get it opened but to warn. You shot the lock. The door opened and you were in sporting goods, amongst the ski-wear.

You shushed the sales clerks. Everyone respected you, even though you kept the gun out of sight. You emerged a ski-person. If you'd had the time you'd have paid for the suit, it fit so well. You looked before exiting the broad glass front door to civilian-land, you did everything right, the coast was clear. You opened the door and forgot, you ran and did not walk and did not watch where you were going. You collided with a policeman, not looking where he was going. The sound of the gun hitting the sidewalk was like a slap on the ear.

v v v

You said you had no explanation. Mr. Delta wanted one. You couldn't give it, no more than you could live on the outside without having some kind of edge, some kind of hedge against punishment, poverty and pain. You stole to be normal, like breathing.

Mr. Delta said again:

"God, you've got brass. Harness that and you'd be unbeatable."

Then why did you just feel beat? Dead tired. Beat.

v v v

But you got it up again in a split second and you saw your chance, the garbage truck leaving, to live again if for just moments and escape an inescapable prison just like in a movie you once saw. It worked because you can do most anything you put your mind to in the pull of a moment, everybody says so and you know it so what's the problem? There you fly out of the garbage but what now? Wander around the dump in your prison greens, trying not to be mistaken for what's all over the place? Finally someone says, Hey, and you give yourself up, dazed, because there was no plan. Only excellent execution.

And dazed is how Delta looks when next he sees you years later and you're still not even near to being out or real again, but you're still doing exercises. Delta says he misses you, a stand-up crook, and you ask what he's doing to keep his gut down and then you say:

99

"Maybe it's because I'm Irish."

So Delta brings you a book about the Irish and you read it but you still don't understand.

The sky opens and you're out again but never a free man. Now the air and especially the clouds weigh heavy on you because, hey, you're not such a young man anymore. Cloudy days make you crazy and you can't believe you're turning into a bug case, the thing you always hate, you can't be like one of those, goof-eyed and drooling. And this time it takes no time at all despite yours and Delta's best efforts but on this go-round you work alone and the first gas station you hit there's a guy coming out of the back with a shotgun and so you shoot and he shoots. You take cover correctly and shoot back again and again and eventually, because you knew what you were doing, you win and he loses. But you just had to live that one time, maybe the last time but it was a time you could breathe and all the air went in and you felt like you had enough.

So now you're back forever and the world is a patch of sky above the wire. And you're happy in a way, but mystified. And Delta talks to you, trying to figure. He says:

"I couldn't help you. What could I do?"

And you say: "I don't know."

And the mirror says you're still a good-looking red-hair, square-jaw and you say to Delta:

"But you still like me, dontcha?" Trying to be flip. Trying to be funny.

And Delta looks sad like he always does nowadays and maybe he always looked that way, can you remember when he didn't? He takes the pencil out of your hand and the string you're making slip-knots with, and sad as he looks, he still says:

"Yes. I still like you."

8

Robert "Bertie" Finwell once offered Barry Delta a handgun.

Parole officers don't carry these things in Canada, a fact Bertie Finwell was aware of, being the long-time jail-clubber he was.

"It's a clean piece," Bertie said. "Thirty-eight Special. Bought it in Montana when I was workin' down there."

"Uh huh."

"For you, three-fifty. Solid. The crazies you got, you need this chunk, man. Really."

"No thanks." Barry once-overed the sweaty apartment as nonchalantly as he could. "But interesting. Is it here?"

"Guy's holding it for me."

That was as far as it went. Barry didn't usually get this kind of thing from ex-bank robber, druggie types with barely a month left on parole, but it was not so unusual in Bertie's case. The man had a rep for mouth-shooting, as well as other kinds of shooting. And by itself it was nothing, not nearly enough to cause trouble. Still, Barry looked at a file as soon as he got back to the office.

v v v

The parole office had a new temporary receptionist. She was twenty-five, wore tight skirts, painted her nails, and immediately made Barry forget about Bertie or anyone else on his caseload. Un-missable was an air of ripeness, a tangible aura, like a smell. It was powerful musk for the single men in the vicinity and she was only staying for a week so they had to work fast. On the same afternoon both the much-experienced office seducer, Daniel C. Perkins, and dark-horse Don Juan, Barry Delta, asked her out. Despite their liberal leanings, their awareness of the right things in the world, the due respect they tried to engender for the rising female status, they were still, when exposed to the stimulus, hounds to the scent. Jocelyn was her name.

Unfortunately, "Dapper" Dan struck first, by five minutes. He got Friday night. Barry accepted Saturday. In serious discussions with John, Barry expressed his uneasiness at having "second up" behind Perkins.

"Bad stroke." John was puffing on one of his obnoxious brown cigarettes, the smoke strung from his nostrils like dirty shoelaces. "That gal's spinny as candy floss. She'll be beddin' the first who buys her a drink with a flower in it."

"Great. Maybe she'll go for both of us."

John scowled, pulling the stick from his teeth. "Now Barry, that's no way to talk. Goin' defeatist on me all of a sudden."

Barry usually consulted with John on matters of woman-chasing. He was always careful what to observe and translate. John was exactly thirty-five years older than him and, though fond of saying things like "Hell, the older you get the wider your choice becomes. You can screw 'em from seventeen to seventy...", sometimes showed a thrilling tenderness and respect toward those women he *did* have relations with. It was a matter of listening closely, separating the macho-bravo bullshit from the sensitive life-love the old man seemed to have for well-rounded man-woman relationships. There seemed to be a place for both attitudes within John's philosophy, as well as a serious respect for the mental health benefits of frequent sexual intercourse.

John turned to the paperwork on his desk, a practical-minded expression firming his face. "Get to work on something," he said gravely. "Don't give up..."

Barry made a last visit to Bertie Finwell. Things had gone well. Four more weeks and it would be all over. Finwell hadn't completed a full term of parole in three previous tries, and was exuberant at the notion of finally flatting one out. "How 'bout it, huh!" he quipped to Barry, who sat with his back to the wall on a decrepit kitchen chair.

"Pretty good. Nobody thought you'd do it. I'm proud of you."

"You helped, man ..." Bertie was a picture of relaxation, sitting with his back on a couch and his feet up on a cluttered, cigarette-rutted coffee table. "No shit. But look, how long I got to go? Exactly."

"I think it's next month, the twentieth."

"One month."

"One whole month. Gonna make it?"

"Look, ah ... How serious are you guys about where I live? I mean, if I was to move, say, next week. Would I have to tell you?"

"Says in the Rule Book, yeah."

"How crazy are you on the Rule Book?"

"Not much. You've been good. Go ahead. Tell me where you end up but I won't write it down or anything."

"Your word?"

"Guaranteed."

"Thanks."

"No problem. I won't ask why."

"Good."

"There is one thing, though." A small, evil idea poofed into his head. It was so perfect he didn't have time to self-debate the morals of it. "There's this guy ..." he said.

"Yeah?"

"Funny dude. You talk about your car fanatics. This guy's got a custom '67 Beaumont two-door he's just nuts about. Perfect shape. Keeps it inside all winter."

"Kinda man I can respect ..."

"And you wouldn't be wrong. Solid, stand-up guy. Good with the ladies. Only thing that could stir him would be something happening to his car. He'd flip. I'll bet if he was out with some girl and something happened to his car, like, it disappeared or something . . . Hell, even if she was Playmate of the month, he wouldn't even be able to get a hard-on, you know? I mean it's that bad."

"I know the type of guy you're talkin' about."

"You do?"

"Sure. You do something to his car, fuck, terminal soft dick-itis, you know?"

"Right . . ."

"Something like that happened to me one time. I know."

"The thing is, he's taking some babe out this Friday . . ."

" . . . uh huh . . ."

" . . . and it would be interesting to see just what his reaction might be. You know?"

"Right."

"If the type of man exists or was around that could get certain risky things done he'd be the man to put on this one. I mean, it's small. Might only mean driving a car a couple of blocks somewhere. But it would have to be clean. Tight."

"No traces, as they say."

"Right. The guy would have to know that the thing was taking place at the Old Portugal on Kingsway sometime after eight-thirty. He'd have to know the car . . ."

" . . . not five others like it in the city . . ."

"Nevertheless, he'd have to know it was the colour blue, with a vanity plate on it that says DAPPER . . ."

"He'd be sure to get it then."

"Good." Barry rose again. "Hope I never see you again, Bertie. Have a nice life."

"Thanks. I'll try."

Barry Delta left, trying not to think too hard about it all.

All Friday afternoon Barry goofed off near the reception desk, trying to cement a good impression. Jocelyn enjoyed it, he could tell, and said she was looking forward to their date tomorrow night. She avoided any mention of her schedule that evening, directing the conversation toward their own proposed activities. Barry mentioned the Bombay Room of the Asian Court Hotel. The girl was enthusiastic: "Ooh, I love it there. They put orchids in the Planter's Punch!"

v v v

Barry had nothing on for the evening so, edgy, he worked out at the gym until almost nine, got something to eat and went home. He hoped he would sleep. He sat in bed watching the news. The phone rang. A voice asked for him, the sounds in the background told him it was the desk officer at the police lock-up.

"We got one of yours. Finwell, Robert."

"Right," said Barry, getting out of bed.

A plainclothesman waited at the desk. He approached when Barry identified himself.

"We been working a buy-and-bust operation all week," he said, "Finwell's been active."

"Junk?"

"Yup."

"No kidding. A step down for him. Usually it's banks."

"That's what we thought, but there it is. We popped him tonight in a stolen car. At least we think it's stolen. It doesn't belong to him. Anyway, it's his type of wheels, flashy and oldish. Nice car."

"That it?"

"We got a small amount on him. That plus our undercover work should do him. Can we get warrants off you?"

"Sure, for all the good it'll do. He's only got a month left."

"Well, we don't want to tip just yet. We'll use your paper, keep our stuff back, lean on him awhile and see if we can't get

105

something. Ask him a few questions about the car. Maybe there's something we can use."

"Uh huh . . ."

" . . . Taking it apart right now."

"What . . . ?" Barry's tongue felt like fried liver. "The car?"

"Yeah. See what's in it."

"Good idea."

"Wanna see him?"

"No thanks," said Barry.

Saturday never went slower. Barry tried not to shit too many bricks over the thing but, dammit, this was serious! No telling what kind of shitstorm might come down if Bertie cracked. Professional disgrace at best. Criminal charges likely. To say nothing of the bodily harm he'd have coming when Dapper Perkins got the drift of what happened . . .

Don't panic, Barry told himself, Bertie's been up against it before. He's one of the best around for keeping his mouth shut when it counts. Look at all those times he took it for his old lady. Or was that just talk? You should know, Delta, you're the so-called professional. Shit! The way things were nowadays, you never knew. Stand-up, solid crooks were getting harder and harder to find. What was the matter with the world! Barry lay in his bathtub, thinking. The water got cold. He almost forgot about the date.

v v v

"So," Barry took a hard slug from the double scotch in his hand. Drunk, the sooner the better, he thought. "How's things?" He looked into her sea-green eyes.

"Fine," she said. There was no hint of strangeness, no clue about her feelings on what might have happened to her in the last twenty-four hours.

106

v v v

No matter how much he drank, Barry could not feel it. The panic of the situation with Bertie was like an illness. The fear, a tangible thing in the centre of his chest, would not go away. He expected the black shadow of a policeman to appear over his shoulder any minute. Jocelyn's eyes would cloud over, alarm on her face, a firm hand would grip his shoulder.

"I'm having a wonderful time," she said.

She sure seemed to be. They watched the goofy Mandarin floorshow at the Asian Court and then, keeping with the Far East mood of the evening, went for sushi in a place where the food floated by on little bamboo boats. "Ooh," she cooed at one point, "I bet they give us the bill on rice paper!"

"No doubt," said Barry.

Later on, when the Japanese beer was finally making progress with his head, Barry realized things were going extremely well for the minimal effort he was putting in. Jocelyn was clinging easily to a contagious cheeriness that, along with the beer, was penetrating his tense gloom. In fact, she was becoming downright delightful. She had yet to say a word about the previous night.

"Coffee?" he asked her, after the raw fish.

"No thanks."

"Well. I'm feeling pretty good. This food always does that. You feel full but light. How 'bout you?"

"Lovely. I hate for it to end."

It was about eleven thirty. Barry hadn't planned anything beyond now and hadn't been paying enough attention to know what to safely suggest for later. He mulled it a second. She took up the thread.

"You said you have a place with a view. Willing to show it?"

"Sure. If you're not too tired."

"I'm fine," she said.

You certainly are, thought Barry.

They paid the rice paper check and left.

107

At his building, Barry wondered if the official-looking unmarked Chevrolet parked down the street was what he thought it was. His breath came short as he imagined himself being arrested at the door in company with this sweet girl. But this did not happen. His hallway was clear.

He showed Jocelyn his place; she giggled and played with his telescope, trying to find a boat on English Bay with enough lights to see in the blackness. "Your place is cute," she said, sitting beside him on the couch. "You and your telescope are cute."

"Thanks."

She shifted on the couch, bringing her legs in front of her, waving them past his face. There was that musk again. Barry wondered if it was natural or manufactured and sold in a bottle. It was directly responsible for the tightening in his crotch, he could swear. He opened some wine, poured two glasses, clinked with hers and they drank.

"Well," he said, shifting.

"Well. I'm glad I'm out with you tonight and not with who I was last night. Ugh . . . "

"Oh . . . ?"

She set her lips, doubtful. "Maybe I shouldn't tell you, but . . . " There was an eagerness. Barry felt like it might relate to his luck for the future of the evening. Jocelyn glowed. He thought it might be the wine getting to her.

" . . . Oh well," she said.

"Doesn't matter . . . "

She began: "No, but . . . Anyway. You may not know it, I went out with Danny Perkins last night."

"Yeah? Where'd you go?"

"He took me to some kind of Spanish place on the east side. It was okay, but he was a dip."

"What . . ?"

"He went on and on about all the places he'd been and seemed to always want to talk over my head and then he went on and on about his car. Have you seen his car?"

"The old one?"

"Yeah. You'd think it was a Rolls Royce or something. Big deal. I look for something else in my men. He took a rag and started shining it in the parking lot. It was so embarrassing. Then he tried to impress me with all this Spanish he was speaking to the people there and then, worst of all, he got up and started dancing around to the music. They were playing this totally grody Spanish stuff that I didn't like but he seemed to think was some kind of fabulous love music or something. Then he orders another bottle of wine when I'd already had enough and starts to drink like a fish and act really embarrassing . . . "

"Goodness."

"Then he wants me to get up and dance with him and I go 'No way, buddy' and he gets all huffy. He says 'You're lucky you're with me because some of the men around here wouldn't take that from a woman.' Well, I just got up and told him I was leaving and he had the nerve to say 'Come on, baby, we gonna go to bed or what?'"

"Unreal . . . "

"Did you know he was like that? I mean, nobody told me."

"I never heard of him pulling something like that. Ol' Dapper's pretty wild they say, but I wouldn't know, really . . . "

"Well anyway, I left and he stayed. I never want to see him again. I'm glad I'm just a temp."

"Yes."

They drank. They talked. After a while she put her hand on his, he put his hand on her neck and drew her close. They kissed, talked some more and kissed again. They spoke of the dancing, the food, themselves, other people, safe sex, and movies. Barry drifted on the wine and kisses, and tried to put Bertie and the disassembled DAPPER '67 Beaumont out of his head. Every time a car went by on the street, he could not resist listening for its stop, footsteps to come. None did. The clock-radio on Barry's bedside table said 03:08 when they kneeled on the bed, peeling each other's clothes.

Her body felt like the perfect place to be. He kissed her deep, she parted her legs, he reached and spread her open, feeling the wet. A belligerent sound boomed through the wall; heavy footsteps, two sets, hurrying up the stairwell next to the bedroom and opening the heavy door in the hall. Barry froze, waiting for the knock. He could have sworn the steps ended at his door. His fingers stayed at her wet-soft place. The knock did not come.

"Yes," she whispered.

Barry was in a sea of good, her slippery-ness, hot in his hand. But he couldn't. Maddening, with Bertie's cell door un-erasable in his head, he could not. With his eyes he saw Heaven with green eyes and a mouth. In his mind were several cars, policemen, heroin. They would not go away. Sighing, he quit the effort, hoping things would develop in time.

v v v

Barry's flaccidity broke with a police-free dawn. He smiled. The receptionist smiled through half-closed eyes. He wondered what kind of man he'd be if he walked around with a .38 Special.

One Thing That Angers Barry Delta Is Having To Fit Into the Cracks.

He knows that someone has to do it but worries about the future, when the cracks might get too wide and he might lose his shape. His elasticity will go and he'll be the permanent general recollection of all that he has compromised, eased and arbitrated: No shape at all.

9

Crown Prosecutor Clive Bettors phoned Barry Delta in the middle of a busy afternoon.

"Barry?"

"Clive. How ya doin', boy?"

"Fine."

"Naw. You never do fine. Something must be wrong."

"I feel something coming on."

"Atta boy . . . "

"Talking to you, it always happens."

"Clive! Is that any way to be?"

Clive and Barry were old school friends. They'd even bunked together one year in university, before the party-factor got to Barry, and the lure of big money and prestige drew Clive into the serious halls of law school.

"Wanna play some racquetball?" asked Barry.

"You kidding? Who's got time?"

"Lawyers. So serious . . . "

It had been a while since their last lunch, racquetball date or anything resembling a social outing. Barry hadn't noticed their gradual drifting, and realized he didn't care that much. For Clive it was a matter of dignity; Barry was often entirely too cheerful, babbling on about all the fun he was having, dating all kinds of women. And therein lay the problem: As the years went by, Clive had begun to lose his hair. He sensed that the increasing shine on

112

his head put a distance between himself and everybody, particularly women. It had been gradual, Barry certainly hadn't mentioned anything. But the feeling wouldn't go away, and his social life had withered in direct proportion to the disappearance of his upper foliage.

"If you wanna do lunch you're too late," Barry said on this day. "Already had mine."

"Are you kidding? I haven't broke for lunch in five years. Lunch is for guys like you, guys with time on their hands."

"Hmm . . . . This is beginning to sound ugly."

"Damn right. Just got the stuff on Patterson."

"Patterson. Davey Patterson?"

"That's the one."

"Hate to tell you, Clive, but if you want to prosecute him you're a little late. Guy's been dead for months . . . "

"I know that. The cops just sent the documents down to archives. I worked on that case. I wondered what happened."

"Yeah. So . . ?"

"You should've held on to that guy when you had the chance. He screwed up and you let him off and look what happened . . . "

"Clive, nobody knows what happened. With Davey or his girlfriend. I think some big boys inside decided they didn't like him or something."

"I'm not talking about how he died. I'm talking about how he lived. Going around with a knife, attacking citizens . . . "

"Hold on. Wayne Stickner isn't exactly what you'd call a citizen."

"Stickner . . ?"

"He's the 'citizen' Davey supposedly attacked. Nothing to get excited about. A case of scuz-rat fighting scuz-rat, believe me. You've heard of the Rummy Bandit?"

"Irrelevant. What I've got in front of me is a good case for attempted murder. Aggravated assault at the very least. Why wasn't I told about this?"

"Talk to the cops. They were sitting on it for future blackmail purposes or something. I don't know."

"They show us what they want to show us; you know that. That's why I depend on you, Barry. You're supposed to circumvent this kind of stuff. Letting a potential murderer go free. I'm right pissed, I hope you know."

"I know."

"Good."

"It was a tough case, Clive."

"I'm bleeding all over."

"Aw, you're still peeved about that legal secretary. That's it, isn't it?"

"Irrelevant again."

"Come on. You had it for her. You missed. That's what it was."

"I didn't miss. Everything was going great until she got a look at you and decided she wanted a guy with hair. That's what it was."

"Come off it, boy. You're not that bald. You coulda nabbed her in half-an-hour if you really put your mind to it. A little bald patch never hurt anybody in that game."

"It's not so little any more. Anyway, that's not what I wanted to talk about and I've been on the phone too long as it is. I'm warning you. No more of this law-unto-yourself kick. You'll find your ass up on a procedural inquiry. Understand?"

"That's tough talk from a bald guy."

"Don't ask me for it, Barry. I'm hot. I'm overworked and underloved. I feel like doing nasty things sometimes. Don't get in the way . . ."

"Whoa . . . Must be bad."

"It's bad."

ᵛ ᵛ ᵛ

Bad or not, Barry Delta had heard enough over the years about Clive's hang-ups. He wouldn't be bothering his mind about it.

114

Barry had seen Clive in court many times. He was good on that score. There were times Barry was very glad they were usually on the same side. He dreaded ever going up on a charge himself and facing Clive on the other side of the courtroom. On that note, friends or not, Clive's threat of procedural inquiry was not idle talk. He quietly thanked fate the Patterson case was dead.

v v v

But two days later Barry Delta got a phone call that put he and Clive back working together again. It was from the Sally Crowshaw house, a halfway facility for female releasees, a place Barry housed his occasional female parolee before they went completely back to drugs and/or prostitution or whatever it was that kept them. Ellen, an alcoholic burnout Barry'd had on his caseload for three months, had come in late from a weekend pass, sobbing and half drunk.

Barry went immediately to the house, was led by a worker to a quiet, dark basement room, the only place in the house with privacy enough to interview, and was left alone with Ellen. She sat on the edge of a tired and stained old couch, weeping gently into a limp kleenex.

"So they called you, huh?" She looked at him through tear-sticky eyes. "Didn't take 'em long . . . "

"They're gonna kick you out of this place, Ellen."

"Fine. I don't care." She turned again to her wet tissue.

"I care. Where am I going to put you?"

"Doesn't matter."

She sniffed and began a jag of serious crying, out of control, shivering and convulsive. Different from the booze-delirium Barry had seen often enough. She went on for some minutes, and reached for his knee with a damp hand. Barry stiffened, but let it sit. She looked like she'd need all the care he could afford to give her. If it meant touching, maybe holding an arm around her for awhile, well, that was probably okay.

"Take it easy," Barry said after a while. "Tell me what's the matter?"

"It's awful . . ."

"What's awful?"

"Everything. I'm gonna be dead soon. I dunno. It doesn't matter."

"You're not making much sense."

ᵛ ᵛ ᵛ

Ellen had been relatively old, sixteen, when her stepfather kicked her out for the final time, for refusing to fellate him while he watched the 1962 World Series on his brand-new black and white television. They'd had fights over this sort of thing before.

Thus socialized, Ellen grew callouses in the right places and quickly worked her way to a respected place on the streets, whoring her way to a fine living for a good number of years.

As must happen in a tale like Ellen's, slow disaster and quick doom in the form of booze and life-sucking temporary lovers brought her down. The summer of her thirty-ninth birthday, Ellen woke up from a three-month bender to find herself married to a lumberjack, living somewhere in the god-awful boonies, trying to act natural in the close world of a secluded logging camp.

Ellen and her husband fought. There were few good times. They had little in common, though they shared a weakness for alcohol. One weekend they both got drunk as usual and fought as usual but unlike usual Ellen alone woke up Monday morning. Bleary-eyed, tired and miserable, but alive. Ellen's husband was not alive. He lay on the bed, staring heavenward, a butcher knife poked from his ribs, only five of its twelve inches showing to the light of day.

At her trial, ageing, still sort-of-sexy Ellen played the pitiful fallen woman; citing liquor, fighting, and marriage as the foes. "I fell asleep and when I woke up he was dead. Lying there," she pleaded. It worked. From murder down to manslaughter and the judge gave her six years. The time took more out of her than she thought it would. This was different than the seven- or ten-day stretches she was used to in her soliciting and vagrancy days. She came out of prison into a changed world, hostile to the past-it hooker who'd lost just about the last of her looks washing cellblock floors.

There was no good reason in Ellen's life to quit booze; it was that simple. Many people did not understand this. Her first two PO's didn't: they quickly sent her back when it became clear to them that they would be babysitting still another hopeless, slobbering drunk through the inevitable downfall to snivelling death. Much better to work on heroin addicts, at least they usually smelled better. But Barry, once getting to know her, sensed in Ellen something in its raw form that he was not finding in other women he knew. A tangible, sensuous pulse. She had a sweet mainline of uncut femininity in her. Barry despaired at the waste, but found himself enjoying her company, and wished very much to protect her.

v v v

"I gotta say something," Ellen said, sniffling. "But I can't say it. It's hard. I need a deal. Protection or something."

"Protection."

"Yeah. The cops or something. I'm gonna die . . . "

"What . . ?"

"Never mind . . . "

"We're not getting anywhere, Ellen."

She looked up from her weeping. "Is there anybody in the hallway?" She looked toward the half-open door. "Make sure there's nobody out there."

"What for?"

"I gotta talk. You're the only one that gets told."

Barry shrugged, got up, looked in the hall, closed the door and sat back down.

"You're not gonna believe this," said Ellen, putting her hand back on Barry's knee. "There was a murder, and I know who did it."

"A murder."

"That's right."

"Well, do the cops know . . ?"

"Yeah, yeah . . . . They already found the body."

"They did."

"Yeah."

"Well, when did it happen? The weekend?"

"No, no . . . . It happened a long time ago. Months. Half a year—"

"Half a year . . . ?

"Yeah."

"You knew about this half a year ago . . . ?"

"No. No. For chrissakes, Barry, let me tell it. I'm level this time. I swear. Why else would I talk like this? I'm not a rat. This thing's got me scared. You know I'm not a rat."

"Yeah, yeah, relax. You're not a rat, Ellen. But you're pretty mixed up. What were you drinking?"

"Everything."

"When did you stop?"

"Last night. Or this morning. I woke up. I had to get out of there, Barry. I even left my purse."

"Get out of where?"

"This guy's apartment. Or at least he says it's his. But none of the clothes in the closets fit him. He's living out of a duffel bag. And there's a big blood-spot on the living room floor he hasn't even tried to clean up. So I believe him, Barry, even though he was drunk, I believe him. He says he killed a guy."

"Wait a minute, back up . . . You say a guy confessed a killing? Right to you? Just for the heck of it?"

"I don't know. He was drunk. Really drunk. Like three-bottles-of-vodka-from-lunch-to-supper drunk. Sober drunk, like the worst ones get. You know . . . "

"I know . . ."

" . . . And we were playing around. He picked me up on the Friday I got the pass and took me to his place and just wanted to fool around for a while, you know. He was pretty good."

"Good. You mean like . . ."

" . . . Like for a guy of fifty-five or sixty or so he was pretty good. Pretty up there. You know . . ."

"Was this a pro date for you or just hanging around . . ?"

"Hah. You flatter me, young boy. At my age you go for the fun if there is any."

"So there was fun."

"You're not kidding. But not once the booze started. Then he just got kind of quiet. Crazy-like quiet. Lookin' at me with those ugly big eyes like some kind of bug or something."

"So you're just hanging around. Waiting for him to sober up."

"No. No. He kind of told me. He said he needed somebody around to clean up. The place was kind of dirty. And he gave me cash to go out and get groceries and things like that. It was kind of nice for awhile. But then he started the bad drinking and I kind of got suspicious . . ."

"The clothes. The blood spot . . . "

"Yeah, and all the money lying around. He could just peel off the C-notes and it didn't look like he worked or anything. I asked and he got all huffy, said he'd been a wheel twenty years ago, made lots of money. Still had plenty of it, too, he said. Then I asked him about the clothes, they were all for a man at least a foot shorter and fifty pounds lighter, and he didn't use any of 'em. That made him real mad and he started roughing me around a bit. But that made him remember what I was around for so I didn't mind so much . . ."

"The fun was coming back into the relationship . . . "

"Make jokes all you want, dearie, but that's how I found the blood-spot. We rolled around on the carpet and this little throw-rug got all bunched up and when I went to put it back I saw it. Scared the piss right out of me. He saw me run to the can and

119

figured out what happened and ran after me shouting that he was going to kill me. I locked the door of the bathroom and that seemed to stop him. He started talking again about how he needed somebody to take care of him and how he liked me and all that. I wouldn't come out of the bathroom until he told me what that spot was about and all those clothes and he seemed to take it okay. He seemed to *want* to tell me. He said he'd known the guy who's apartment this was but had got drunk with him one night and lost his temper and killed him. Just like that. He said he kind of understood why it happened because, he said, there'd been a time when he'd just kill a guy for any reason, for business or whatever and it got so easy that now the instinct was still with him. That was how he said it, instinct. Like an animal. I was sitting on the can, crying my eyes out and he was pleading with me to open the door but I was scared shitless, you know? But after awhile I could hear it in his voice that he was really trying to control himself and he really wanted me to understand, like. So I finally got up enough guts to open the door and we had another drink and talked some more and even fooled around again. But later he got drinking a lot more and got those staring, dead eyes like a snake and started growling about how he couldn't let anybody know what he had done. Sort of roundabout telling me he was going to have to kill me for knowing what I knew. Scared me shitless again but I managed to fill him full of drinks and fooled around with him some more and he finally fell asleep. Funny, eh? I took off this morning, he was sleeping so dead I knew he wouldn't hear me. But he knows where I live and he'll be hot like crazy when he wakes up so I gotta get out of here, Barry, I gotta go somewhere else where he won't find me."

Ellen's hand had tightened on Barry's knee. He took the hand in his, peeled it off, held it and said: "Don't worry. They're kicking you out of this place anyway."

v v v

Which was why Barry didn't get around to checking on Ellen's story right away. He had to find another flop for her, one acceptable to her, the flop itself, and him. Least of all him. In the end he stashed her at the Catholic Charities hostel with the promise that it would only be for a few days. Ellen's reputation was well established around town. Nobody wanted her.

So it was a day later that Barry started looking through the police bulletins of six months ago and discovered right away that an unclothed, unidentified male body had been found washed up on Crescent Beach. The police were very interested when he called: they bid him come downtown right away. The story checked. Barry became something of an attraction among the detectives, sitting at an empty desk with a police coffee in his hand, recounting his part of the story. It was a major break in a murder case that had the police totally stumped. They hid Ellen, interrogated her, double-checked her story, and finally made an arrest. The case was handed to Clive Bettors to prosecute. His first move was to call Barry and chew him out for holding on to Ellen's information for a whole day without taking action.

"You gonna be nasty and hard like this for the duration?"

"If I have to. We're dealing with strange stuff here. More than meets the eye. Mob connections . . . "

"Whee . . . "

v v v

But it was true. The suspect was named Clellan James Hardy. Barry wandered over to John's office one day with little to do and wondered out loud who this man Hardy really was.

"Hardy. Hardy . . . " John sat back in his noisy swivel chair and, predictably, lit a cigarillo. "Clellan Hardy. Strange name, Clellan. Irish or something isn't it?"

"Dunno. Got his picture right here."

Barry showed John a photo taken from the police bulletin. John sat slowly upright, taking the cigarillo out of his mouth.

"This is Jim Hardy. Never used the first name. Used to work at the rail yards back about twenty years ago . . . "

"You know him?"

"Just the reputation. Bad one. Thought he was dead."

"No kidding . . . "

" . . . Bad guy. That's for sure."

"How so?"

"Used to work ostensibly as a charge-hand sectionman. But this bastard never knew a spike from a pick handle in his life. He was the union boss's muscle. Saw him break some heads once. Bad guy. Not our sort at all. Never got caught. Rumoured to have killed some guys."

"That's what Ellen says."

"Believe her."

ᵛ ᵛ ᵛ

Clellan James Hardy was arrested and charged, and a date for preliminary hearing was set. Ellen became the main Crown witness in what was a relatively big case, big enough for the government to grant her protection if necessary. Once apprised of this fact, she outrightly demanded it. Plus money, too. The police department assigned two detectives, Alan and Dave, to the job of making sure she made it to the trial in one piece. Barry, ever interested, and still responsible for Ellen from the parole end of things, volunteered his help.

"No thanks," said Dave over the telephone. "I think we got things in hand. Thanks anyway."

"Suit yourself." Barry could not help but note the condescension in the cop's voice. Not many cops had much use for parole people. "We catch 'em, you let 'em go," they'd simplistically say.

122

But two days later the tune changed. Dave phoned Barry: "Look, ah . . . . We got a problem."

When Barry got to the house they were using to keep her, Ellen had just finished setting fire to a set of thick curtains. Alan opened the door for Barry, who couldn't help noticing the policeman's sweat and smoke-stained shirt. "She phoned for a goddamn bottle," said Alan, stepping aside to let Barry in. He held a dripping fire extinguisher in one hand.

"Who gave her money?"

"The government. That Bettors guy. Said give 'er what she wants. Keep 'er happy. This broad doesn't get happy. Keeps askin' for you."

"Oh yeah?"

"Can't figure it," said Alan, his eyes following Barry's closely, suspicion as plain on his face as soot. "You're not doing anything funny with her, are you kid . . ?"

"Smoke much?" said Barry, moving past Alan.

Ellen slouched on a living room couch, disheveled. Still-steaming piles of scorched draperies lay everywhere.

"They took away my bottle, sweetie. No fair."

"Hi, Ellen. How's things?"

"You gotta get me outta here." She straightened, grabbed Barry's hand and put it to her cheek. "Gonna get me outta here? Baby? Huh?"

"Ellen," Barry gently got back his hand, "you can't call me Baby. It's not professional."

"Okay, sweet little Barry-pie. Whatever you want, baby. But get me out of this place, will ya? I'm gettin' so lonely."

"Is that the problem, Ellen? Are you lonely?"

"Yeah . . . " Her voice was thick with booze and baby sounds, a slurred, sarcastic lullaby.

"We're gonna have to move her out of here," Alan said. "We can't watch her twenty-four hours a day."

"That's what it's going to take. Got any place in mind?"

"We thought you might."

"Well, that's a toughie . . ."

"Barry, sweetie. I'm not a toughie, am I? I'm a sweetie, just like you, aren't I?"

Barry walked her to the bathroom for a shower.

This was all happening at a time when Barry Delta was in a major woman-drought. The best he could get was two weeks worth of rock and roll with a waitress he chatted up one night at his favourite beanery. A nice girl, but spinny, trying fervently to make it as an actress in her spare time. When she lost her job for being too spacey to remember orders the trauma sent her into orbit and Barry eased out.

One Sunday afternoon he was sitting in his apartment sipping wine with an up-and-coming dancer with a local company who part-timed as a clerk in a bookstore. She was a little foul-mouthed, even for Barry, but the girl had a body. He'd often wondered what it would be like to plunder a trained figure like that, and things were going good. This was the second date. But Barry hadn't fully explained his line of work to her yet and, this quiet, inopportune Sunday afternoon, his telephone unfortunately rang.

"Barry, shweetie . . . ."

"Ellen. Not now. Where are you?"

"Where you put me, lovey. I'm behaving . . ."

"Doesn't sound like it."

"Do you love me, Barry?"

"What . . . ?"

"You love me, don't you shweetie . . . Why don't you show it?"

"Ellen, settle down. I'll come see you this afternoon. Don't leave."

"I won't leave. Nowhere to go . . ."

"Who got you the bottle?"

"Nobody . . ."

"Is 'nobody' still there?"

"Barry, sweetie, mmmm, kiss, kiss . . ."

124

"Cut it out, Ellen. Come on now, for your own good. Who knows where you are?"

"Little friend of Ellen's. He won't tell ... "

"We're gonna have to move you. I wish you wouldn't do this. I'm running out of places. It's still two more months 'til the preliminary."

"You love me, don't you Barry-pie ... ?'

"Bye, Ellen ... "

"Love me ... ?"

"Get off the phone. And don't call anybody else."

"Say you love me first. Love me ... ?"

"Bye, Ellen ... "

"Love me ... ?"

"Love you, okay."

"Say you love me, sweetie, it's so lonely here. I can't stand it."

"I love you."

"So lonely ... "

"I love you, Ellen. Hear? You're a loved person."

"You love me?"

"I love you."

"Oh, say it again, baby. Say it more. I gotta ... I need it, baby."

"I love you."

"You love me."

"Yes," Barry said. "I do."

Barry hung up the phone, regretful that he'd broken his no-home-phone-number rule for just this one time. For Ellen. Who needed protection, mostly from herself.

The dancer sat up straight, put her glass down and reached for her shoes, looking at him with distaste.

"You're fucking weird," she said.

v v v

Another busy afternoon. Another Clive Bettors phone call.

"Barry! When're you going to get on-side?"

"What are you talking about, Clive?"

"I just got a call from Alan and Dave. They don't know where our principal witness is! They say you moved her and didn't tell them. Is this true?"

"Shit . . ."

"Should I take that as a yes . . . ?"

"She blew her locale. I had to move her on the weekend."

"Aha. And how long were you going to keep this your own dark secret? What if something happened to you? What then? Would we just wait for her to grab a bus into court?"

"I dunno if I can hold her for another two months, Clive. She's out of control. The cops aren't being much help . . . "

"They've got all the manpower they can spare on it right now. You should see the measly budget for this kind of thing. Damn near nonexistent . . . "

"That doesn't help me . . . "

"You can afford to go the extra mile once in a blue moon."

"Extra mile! You don't know what I've had to give up. Ever made it with a dancer?"

"What . . . ?"

"Forget it . . . . Okay. I'll get onto Alan and Dave right away. Keep them up with things. Anything else?"

"Yeah. The court date. You're gonna have to hold her for three months now, instead of two. Defence waived prelim. We go straight to trial."

"Whoa . . . !"

" . . . You said it."

" . . . an extra month! I'm gonna need a mental health retirement!"

"Oh, settle down."

"Maybe this isn't such a good idea. Maybe we better get somebody else to testify. She might not even remember . . . "

"We got bugger-all for evidence, just your girlfriend. Take good care of her."

"Oh god . . . "

v v v

From then on, Barry had a strangely better working relationship with Alan and Dave. They even took him to lunch and paid the bill. They spoke nicely to him. It occurred to him, whizzing along through traffic, sitting in the back of the unmarked car like some kind of V.I.P., that they were taking care of him so he'd take care of Ellen. They didn't want to get their hands dirty. They were smart, Barry thought.

But something else occurred to him. Maybe the cops knew something he didn't. After all, they'd been doing the investigation. There were supposed to be heavy people involved, although Barry had been told nothing since the case first broke with Ellen's story. Was this thing dangerous? He couldn't tell.

v v v

Though the time went slow, with three more changes of address, the day finally arrived for Ellen's testimony. Barry chauffeured her to the courthouse and dropped her off.

"You're not coming in?" Her voice cracked with worry. Barry had enforced a total drinking ban for the previous week, working very hard to keep her straight. The straighter Ellen was, the more scared she felt.

"I hate courtrooms. Besides, they don't need me. Just you." Barry pointed past her to where three policemen stood by the massive courthouse doors. "There's Dave now."

"Couldn't you just come and hold my hand?"

"Ellen!"

v v v

Barry's morning started slow but got frenetic as it rolled along. Phone calls from irate people. Unexpected visits from errant parolees and others. He was on his way out the door to see one of his charges in a hospital psyche ward when Clive Bettors phoned.

"Get down here."

"I can't right now. Maybe later . . . "

"Right now. They called a recess. She broke down, hysterical. Says she won't go back unless you come and hold her hand. I don't care what else you're doing . . . "

"Look, I got a guy going crazy at Saint Paul's walking around sticking a knife in his arm. I got reports due, phone calls to return . . . Get some doctor to give her a shot or something."

There was silence from Clive's end. When he spoke again his voice was low and threatening. "Maybe I'm not making myself quite clear."

v v v

Barry was startled at the sight of Lance Pithorn for the defence. He leaned close to Clive's ear, whispering.

"Fucker's got the best lawyer in the country! Who's the money behind him?"

"I don't know. Must have a stash. If I had time to find out stuff like that I wouldn't be losing my hair."

"You mean you haven't looked?"

"Looked at what?"

"His bank accounts! You gotta know where his money comes from. We could be playing with a lot bigger stuff here than we think."

"Barry, the guy's a drunk who got violent. That's it. And relax. We got the goods on him, no problem."

"Oh, so now the tune changes. He's a drunk now. What about all that Mob shit you were chucking at me a while back?"

"What about it?"

"Well it seemed to mean a lot to you at the time. All this witness protection stuff . . . "

"It did mean a lot. It's the only way we could ever get this guy."

"Okay then. On a case like this you should have a team going at it. I mean, how often do you get one of these organized crime guys in your sights, anyway?"

"Look, Barry. You know it and I know it that the guy's guilty and he was probably a connected person at one time or another. But knowing it and proving it are two different things. In the meantime, we've got to prosecute this case like any other drunken fight murder story. That's all our witness can give us . . . "

ᴠ ᴠ ᴠ

Ellen's testimony and cross examination lasted seven-and-a-half hours over two days. For most of it, Barry Delta sat close by, looking at her, nodding, smiling encouragement. Keeping a supply of kleenex handy. For all of that time, whenever he chanced a look, Barry could see Clellan James Hardy and he knew Hardy was looking at him.

Looking is a mild word. Hardy was a tallish man, thin and gray-haired, with the hardest, deepest chasm-eyes Barry had ever seen. You couldn't miss them even if he wasn't looking at you. Hardy glared with disdain at Clive Bettors. His aside glance at his own lawyer was non-committal. His stare at Ellen was resentful but with a certain resigned affection. But for Barry, coaching and cajoling Ellen on to a grisly, patchwork-picture of the crime, Clellan James Hardy, reputed former button-man for union bosses, had a look murderous and coolly reptilian. It was like staring into the eyes of a boa constrictor. Barry was unnerved. No matter how many times he caught it, Barry could not get used to that look. There was no mistaking the message. It said: "I'll get you, punk!" Late in the morning of the second day, as Ellen was close to finishing, Barry collected his wits, turned to Hardy and, blurring his eyes so he wouldn't actually see the man, gave him his best "Not if I get you first, motherfucker!" expression.

v v v

Ellen held together well once Barry was there. When Clive finished his questioning, Lance Pithorn rose and quietly, coolly went about his cross-examination. Having seen that Ellen could easily break down, he was careful not to jostle her too hard, at least not until he could detect where the real weaknesses of her story lay. Barry detected right away that Lance Pithorn knew where he was going with her.

"You have testified," he said to Ellen, "that the defendant told you everything about the alleged murder. Did he tell you exactly how he went about the killing?"

"He strangled the guy. That's what he said. They had kind of a fight."

"A fight, yes. We know that the victim had several scalp wounds, but actually died of strangulation. Now, the defendant said to you, in his own words, 'I choked him', or 'I strangled him', or words to that effect. Is that true?"

"Yes."

"And that was all. He did this alone. With no help. And he disposed of the body, you say, by himself. With no-one aware of what he was carrying down to his car. Is that correct?"

"Yeah. I guess so."

"Thank-you. No further questions, My Lord."

The Judge dismissed Ellen from the rest of the trial and then adjourned the court for lunch. Clive stuffed a twenty-dollar bill in Barry's hand. "Take her to lunch," he said, "and get her back by two. Her flight's at three."

"Where's the cops? I got things to do."

"Busy," said Clive, walking away.

At lunch, sitting in the glass front of a fish and chip shop, Ellen was in a jovial mood.

"It's a new start for me, sweetie. I'm going back East."

"How much did you get?"

"Seventy-five hundred."

"Not bad."

"I wanted ten grand. But Alan said they didn't have the money in the budget. Is that true?"

"I don't know. I guess so. Doesn't seem like much when you figure you probably can't come back here for a long time ..."

"That doesn't bother me one bit, Barry-sweetie."

"Really?"

"Nothing's gone right for me out here. Nothing. That asshole husband of mine ... How I ever got into that mess I'll never know."

"Guess he regrets it too."

"Hah! He's better off, believe me. He was too stupid to know he was miserable."

"Hmmm ... Guess you're both better off ..."

"Bet on it ..."

Ellen leaned close to Barry, and spoke low. "You know, seeing as how they're relocating me and all, I suppose it wouldn't be so bad if we could go to bed together, like we've been thinking ..."

"Hold it, hold it ... What the hell are you talking about?"

"Aw, c'mon, Barry, you know I like you an awful lot. Wouldn't it be great? Wouldn't it? I mean, you've probably never made love with a woman like me. Experienced. Been around. I've done lots of things, sweetie, lots of wild and kinky things. Wouldn't it be nice, huh? Wouldn't you like a little head at least? I'm one of the best—"

"Ellen, stop that. People might hear ..."

"Who cares, I'm going away ..."

"Well I'm not. For crying out loud, have some sense of decorum or something. I'm your parole officer, for goodness sake. Is that any way to talk?"

"Oh, Barry ..." She put her hand on Barry's shoulder. "I could make you feel so good. So good ..."

Barry glanced nervously around, brushing her advance away as inconspicuously as possible.

"You're such a nice little boy. Your momma did a good job. Nice manners. So good looking ... I've never had a man with an education before, at least not that I've got to know. You're so intelligent. I bet you treat women really nice, don't you. Really nice. Flowers. Dinner on the town. You're so cute. I'll bet you don't even fuck on the first date ... "

"Look, watch your language. I'm not going to tell you again."

"Relax, sweetie ... " She leaned close. Barry could smell her decadent, drunk's breath. "I wanna tell you something. Something nobody knows. Promise not to tell."

"I can't promise anything."

"Please ... "

"Don't be silly."

"It won't hurt."

"Oh for godsake ... "

"I'll behave afterward."

"Promise?"

"Surely."

"Okay, anything to stop this. What is it?"

"It's about me. It's special and it's about me. I want you to know. It doesn't matter anyway, there's nothing anybody can do about it, they're sending me away ... "

"What is it?"

"You know why I'm doing time?"

"Of course, you ventilated your old man's chest with a butcher knife. Drunk. And it better not happen again, or the judge won't take that blackout story and you'll be doing a life bit like other killers."

"That's right. It wasn't any blackout. I've got to tell you, Barry, it's no good unless you know. I wasn't blacked out. I wasn't even drunk, 'til after. I waited until he was shit-faced, passed out, and then I got a knife and killed him. Just like that. I'd do it again. It was simple. I'm glad I did it. I'm glad I told you about it. Do you understand, sweetie? Do you know why I had to tell you?"

"I'm not sure."

"If we're not going to be lovers, at least we share something. At least there's that. Eh, Barry?"

"I guess. This is pretty kinky, Ellen. I hope you know."

Ellen laughed. Long and loud.

Barry watched her closely, hoping she would stop without going over the edge into hysteria. There was a certain note in her laugh that warned him of the possibility.

Looking at her, he noticed something. Her eyes, elated and giddy for the first time since he'd known her, had at the same time taken on a strange, fish-like blankness. Just like what's-his-name, Barry thought, just like the other guy. He was glad she wasn't touching him any more.

It came to Barry that for a person possibly wanted by the mob or other persons undesirable, he had Ellen sitting in a vulnerable place. Out in the open. He bit into a piece of fish but did not taste it, even though it was soaked in vinegar. An image—shattering glass, flying, fouling the food, splashing his back like hard rain off a car-roof—formed in his head. He tried to think of other things, but couldn't get it out. It ruined the meal.

Two days later Barry put in a call to Clive at noon hour and was lucky enough to catch him in from court.

"How's it going?"

"Not bad. Almost finished with the physical evidence. Pithorn winds up his witnesses this afternoon. You got any idea why he'd be calling a doctor as a witness?"

"No. Just a straight MD or a shrink?"

"MD. Funny . . ."

"Look, Clive. Nothing personal, but, are you really doing your best on this one? I mean, if I were you, I'd know damn well or at least have a pretty good idea what was up, you know? This is a goddamn murder case. You gotta put that guy away; he's one dangerous son-of-a-bitch, compadre."

"Look who's getting concerned all of a sudden. You know who the victim was?"

"Some small-time goof or something . . . "

"Some small-time crooklette, had a record for bad paper, robbery, nickel-and-dime drugs. General nothing. So who cares, Barry? It's scuz-rat killing scuz-rat. Somebody said that to me one time, who was it? Can't remember . . . "

"Funny boy . . . "

"Yeah, funny."

"Just get back there and convict the fucker, will ya?"

"Makes you nervous, does he?"

"Kinda. Sure. Why not. He killed lottsa guys . . . "

"Do you know that? Do you have proof . . . ?"

"No, I don't have proof. Who needs proof. All you have to do is take one look at the guy. All the proof you need. That's a killer if I ever saw one . . . "

"Relax, Barry . . . "

"Yeah, sure. Relax. Okay, Clarence Darrow, I'll relax . . . "

"I'm hungry. See you later . . . "

"Okay, catch you later, pal. Accent on the *pal*."

"Yeah, pal. Okay."

Clive hung up. Barry fidgeted with the phone, hung it up. He thought to himself: accent on the *catch*.

v v v

The next morning Barry was inhaling his first double cappucino of the day when he turned page nine of the early scandal sheet and learned Clellan James Hardy had been found not guilty of second degree murder in a surprise ending to the trial late the previous afternoon. The brilliant Lance Pithorn had presented one expert witness, Hardy's family doctor, who'd been treating the man for arthritis over many years. In the words of the physician: "Mr. Hardy is a semi-crippled individual. His manual function is acutely impaired. It would have been physically impossible for him to have strangled a bird, much less a human being . . . "

ˇ ˇ ˇ

Clive's phone rang. He knew it was Barry.

"Fuck, Clive! It's gotta be the oldest one around. I think I even saw it on Perry Mason one time . . . "

"It was pretty good . . . "

"Pretty good! There's a murderer walking loose. And he's got it in for me!"

"Don't panic."

"Easy for you to say . . . . Didn't you even try to get a recess or something? Bring in your own expert . . . ?"

"I could have tried, I guess. But the budget, Barry. I was out of money . . . "

"Out of money!"

"And even if I did bring somebody in, we were done for. Ellen's testimony wasn't that great. She came across too much like a retired hooker on the make . . . "

"She *is* a retired hooker on the make."

"That's the problem. Anyway, you win some, you lose some. You wanna play racquetball?"

"Racquetball? Racquetball! I gotta get these cops off my back. They already called me up, saying they think *I* fucked up . . . !"

Clive laughed. He'd never heard fright in Barry's voice before but he'd always suspected it would be there, given the right situation. It was funny to hear, he couldn't help chuckling, remembering why he went into law in the first place.

Barry Delta Was Finally Ordered To Go To A Conference.

He was low on training hours. Barry always had a problem with conferences, seminars, meetings and so forth. He couldn't stay awake. Literally. His eyelids would leaden, he'd falter, catch himself, falter again, and in the end get mad, excuse himself, leave as if going to the washroom, and not come back.

At this conference, quite a few people in the corrections game got up and spoke. Some of them were interesting but Barry barely made it between the coffee breaks. Almost at the end a man got up to the podium who had run the big organization for a few years and then got out. He started his talk by saying: "While I was in the job I felt okay. But now, looking back, I don't know what the hell was going on . . ."

It was one of the few times the words spoken kept Barry awake. He excused himself anyway, saying he had to go to the men's room.

10

The Delta creature once again slashes my soul with it's acidic tentacles.

v v v

"I don't mind saying, Stanley, that I'm surprised, upset, downright disturbed that you're here . . . "

"Why would that be, Mr. Delta?"

" . . . I mean it's truly amazing. The way things were last, with you pasted to the wall in that psyche ward, shrieking something about machine surveillance in your wristwatch, psycho-mechanized-android-spywork by yours truly . . . "

"It was a difficult time, sir . . . "

"I'll tell the world it was difficult all right! On that point we agree. The thing is, how are we going to avoid further, as you say, 'difficult times'?"

"Things will be different this time, sir."

"I can tell by looking at you, just by your facial expression, and by your nervous hand motions and the way you call me mister and sir, that you're still the flat-out wacko that I hauled into the hospital and begged three doctors to certify so you'd stay out of my hair for good. But I guess when you got to Regional Psychiatric you somehow cooked up a plan to get transferred. Probably acted so obnoxious for long enough somebody in security started trying to get rid of you, probably against the best wishes of psychology but no matter, you got yourself kicked over to the prairies and once you were out of province your certification automatically lapsed, so instead of getting dumped on a locked ward when your release date came up they just plopped you on the street with a plane ticket in your pocket. And now you're back here, acting superficially sane so that I could never get the doctors to vote you back into custody, and you're crazy and dangerous as ever, worse maybe, and I'm not fooled by a second of it, my man, so the question, the question is what do we do about it? What do we do to get you into the right care so people are safe to walk the streets around here without fear of some guy slicing their clothes off with a razor blade."

"Your attitude is unprofessional, sir . . . "

"Aw, shut up . . . "

" . . . But you needn't fear an official complaint to your supervisor. I'm not the vindictive kind. I can forgive imperfections. And I'm sure that your job is providing no end of frustration and stress . . . "

"I was doing fine until they handed your file over and said you'd be out by the end of the week."

"As I said, I'm sure we can come to some kind of understanding."

"I'll tell you what I understand, Stanley. I understand that you can't help what you are or what you do. I'll give you that. I have to, because how would I work with you otherwise? How would I handle a guy who actually likes doing the kind of stuff you're supposed to have done in the past, and might well do again in the future, if I didn't think it was some kind of accident of nature, misfortune, mistreatment and loss conspiring against your being a whole human being somehow. Now given that you're an unfortunate man, and not the Devil-incarnate, how do I go about seeing that you're safe for human co-existence? Can you help me out? You're pretty brilliant at times, how would you go about it if you were in my shoes?"

"I . . . I can't imagine being in your shoes, Mr. Delta."

"Okay, quit trying. Just listen. I'm going to see you every single day. Got that? Every day. You will call me daily by ten a.m. Understand? You will telephone me every morning and we will arrange for us to see each other every day. Whenever's convenient for each other, the afternoon, night or whatever, but every day. Understand?"

"Perfectly."

"Another thing. I'm sending you to a doctor. Here's the number. Phone him this afternoon and get an appointment. Be sure to do it. If you haven't done it by the time I see you tomorrow, I'm sending you back. I'm that touchy. Treat me nice. I've got a hair trigger this time around, I'm not taking any chances. You're gonna have to work hard on this, and really do it for yourself. I can't help you except to put you back in jail. Do you understand all this?"

"Quite well."

"If only . . . "

Quite well, I understand quite well, the beast issues its horror-dripping words into my brain, carving its orders in my mind with its dull mental knife. I have little time. Really none at all. The Delta monster wants its evil work done immediately. There is no relenting in its death-lust. I must act now or never fulfil my evil-borne orders. Some day I will learn from whence he gets his incredibly insightful information, I am not fully convinced there are still not electronic listening devices secreted on or in my body. No time to look for them, my assignment is cast.

ᵛ ᵛ ᵛ

Luckily my earlier selection is still available, reading the evil news on the surveillance tube, smiling her awful smile with blood-smeared lips. Delta must have seen her, he must have felt what I feel at her lascivious verbosity, issuing the damning invitations to view and share the profound pornography of human misfortune and depravity. I have not even time to wonder why I am chosen, why I must do what I must do. Why I must ride the public transit in my prison uniform, its artificial fabrics slowly turning to acid and burning my skin, speeding me to my chore, when after it is done I'll have earned easier clothes and perhaps (but what do I hope?) the respect of my monster-master. I post myself outside the massive tubed building with its sinister aerials and many feet walking in and out of its mouth-like entrance. I try not to look at its painfully flashing electric message-board, I am sure there will be orders sent to interrupt my true mission, my destined assignment from the Devil's messenger, whom I cannot disobey, I cannot evade, I fear above all that which is most fearful. The feet come and go for torturous hours until the sun is gone and the flashing sign-board of the media demons intensely attempts to sway me from my task. I have come too far to get so close to final liberation to let as loosely cheap and futile a device control me. I look away, examining the feet, knowing I will know the correct pair when they walk past, knowing what I must do to appease the hair-trigger bomb which must be within me, it must be, controlled by the ugly beyond-life Delta creature who enslaves me with evil control.

v v v

The hours have passed and my strength remains clear, my implement still sharp and hungry. But now it begins to be cold and my shivering is breaking down the hate-matter that fuels my sinful avenger. I am freezing, almost dying as the number of feet passing by dwindles to a silent non-cadence. Am I lost? Was there a flaw in this purpose? Impossible, I know in my liquid black innards. But must there be this doubt, this loneliness in the shivering dark waiting for this ghost?

140

v v v

Finally, I see light-glints from the silent doorway and steps are sounding, clear as though electric-amplified and I see the face, the hands, arms, and the clothing of her, the excellent black silhouette against the glowing face of the glass building. But is it really her which tells the bare-faced indecency of daily humanity? Is it, more evil still, one of her diabolical replica sisters in filth-evil, walking the streets as a normal human but transgressing for the purposes of cursed manipulation, horrible, unappeasable blackness like the demon who holds me in its darkened, despicable sway? No matter, the trail of her scent is a message to me, her clothing-flash in the frigid breeze beckons me as I knew it must when I located the Right One.

v v v

She coyly boards a bus. I follow. Sitting behind her I am almost overcome by her scent-defence, the potency almost sends me to the floor in temporary ecstasy, but I've been controlled in this way before, I cover my smelling gland with a sweat-soaked sleeve of the fast-corrupting polyester jacket. Not for much longer. I see that she wears the exquisite fibres of plants and spinning insects. Excellent. I look forward to exploring her collection: an apt reward for my long journey of physical and psychic incarceration.

v v v

She rises to disembark. I follow discreetly. We walk together, locking into step. As we approach a darkened building I see how the task will be done: her key unlocks the entrance and the sprung door closes reluctantly. This I am prepared for. I have practised waiting until the last possible moment before snatching the almost-latched entrance wide to reveal me, vindicator, having lulled the intended into thinking she is safely home. I see her instantly, perfectly, her hand on the key in her mailbox, her eyes knowing instantly why I am here. Wordless, our dance begins without pause; seamless, the grandeur of it stills the breath in my chest, I seem not to need air, I exist now on the stored energy in my intestines, the engine of black business which I've carried for the years of suffering since my last arrival in this blessed ballroom. It is good to feel the cords of her neck and throat, hard against my fingers, tensing and trying to emerge, her voice sounding only for an instant before her capacity for noise is solidly removed. I twist her key-hand and examine the printed messages within. The apartment number is prominently displayed and therefore confirms to me the rightness of my acquiring this, the target, after so long, and such cold sacrifice. I propel my struggling quarry down the hallway, up stairs, through doors and on to her crucible as if I were made of liquid power, unable to falter in my sacred task, now with all the controlling power so ruthlessly exercised upon me by others every waking hour of every day, save when, like now, I exercise my given special strength. We enter through a door which magically opens with a minimum of fumbling keys, the perfect coordination of my thoughts to action, I further marvel at my control. Her struggles are perfectly token, her attempts to mar my weapon ineffectual.

v v v

Dying angel, you fight so poignantly, so lovely in your desperate ugliness, it will be an honour to change you, to do you unto the controllers and the monsters who would play the world's humans for the puppets we are. But alas, we were not put here, it seems, to order, but to be ordered. I splay her limpening body across the dining room table and tie her limbs to the legs with the strong tape I have prepared myself with. Though I want very much to select the proper blade from her prominently-displayed collection in the kitchen, I am taken by her scent once more and, removing the impediments, insert my primary weapon where it

142

will do the most profound, and experience immediately the welcome and long-expected release of some of the vile poisons and molten evil which exist in my bowels. Blazing, power-flaming into her innards, the craze-juice flies, searing, I can tell, its way into her soul and her life, seating where it will never be un-sat, changing forever her future and erasing her past. I am impressed how quickly and well this preliminary treatment has gone and proceed to the kitchen to select my further implement. It must be proper and clean, to respect this most excellent of hosts. Her eyes have the fear of a goddess; they fill me with comfort. So little of it in my life, and yet she gives of it so freely. The love pours from my eyes to hers and I feel so quiet and at rest that I wish our marriage could remain for all time, and not just this fleeting moment which must come to an end so soon. Carefully, I remove the perfect clothing and do the goddess the honour of opening several appropriate entrances in her torso, being careful not to damage any essential organs or other parts which might shorten her life unduly, and prevent her from enjoying the profound tribute which I will now impart to her. Gently I enter her bowels with my extension, careful not to cause undue interruption of her own rapt experience, easing myself into her as a true lover.

v v v

In the night air, my head crystalline, wearing her soft blouse under the repulsive plastic jacket provided by the authorities, I only hope Delta understands and appreciates.

Barry Delta Knows He Is Not Good With Women.

But what's the point in talking about it? You talk about things you think you can fix, stuff that does not threaten your centre and make you tell lies just to survive.

There have been a number of women. Barry knows he has become artistic about the acquiring. He caresses their hair and fights the sadness he has for them. As with parolees, he talks to them, strokes and cares for them. The problem is after. The crooks all have warrant expiry dates, a time when most of them will go away by statute; nothing solved or explained, but simple.

The women don't have warrant expiry dates. They have to expire themselves some other way.

11

The invitation to Danny Speller's wedding came the same day I rammed the Honda into a bread truck. The bread truck wasn't scratched, but the car got hurt bad. I loaded the mangled bumper into the hatchback and limped over to Danny's backyard garage.

Danny looked at the Honda, grinning. "How'd it happen?" He did not laugh, sensitive to how I was feeling. I was glad nobody was hanging around.

"Aw . . . goddamn truck was in front of me in one of those angle intersections . . . Wasn't looking where I was going. Pissed me off. Not a scratch on the truck . . . "

"Well, we can get this bumper back on," Danny peered under the crumpled hood. "She'll look rough . . . "

"That's okay . . . "

"You should get a new car."

"I should get a lot of things, but I don't. Can you figure it . . ?"

Danny Speller was a old case of mine. In his young and foolish days, he did management-trainee service with a country-wide stolen goods business. That ended with a three year stretch in one of our exclusive resorts. Now he's just a citizen, an all-round nice guy, not to mention a damn good auto mechanic. I enjoyed his company. Hanging around his garage, drinking coffee from dirty cups, gave me that fraternal hang-around-the-local-service-station experience I somehow missed in my teens.

145

"Glad you're here," he said, going for a wrench, "save me giving you a call. I'm gonna get married."

"What . . . ?"

"That's right."

"Well, congratulations. Do I know her?"

"Maybe. While ago. She was here once, brought my lunch."

"Chinese girl?"

"Right."

"Well . . !"

"No kidding . . !"

Danny worked. I peered around, handing him tools, trying to be useful.

"So. Getting married up and everything, Danny old boy. Legitimate up the old whazoo. Pretty soon there'll be a bunch of kids running around here. A real family man. Pretty soon you'll be running for school board . . . "

"Hah, hah . . . "

"No, seriously. This is great. Kind of follows along with your growing up and getting out of the gangs and stuff. Icing on the cake. Pretty soon you'll move out of this end of town and really start new. Congratulations again."

"I don't wanna move out of this end of town."

"Well, I'm only thinking about when you were in trouble . . . "

"Never happen again . . . "

"I know, but . . . . Surrounded by your old buddies . . . "

"I grew up with those guys. I went to school with 'em."

"Exactly. They're never going to let you forget it either."

"Don't worry, Barry. Nothing much happens anymore. They only come around here for advice."

"Advice! They listen?"

"Sometimes. Pass me that big crescent, there . . . " He pointed from under the car up to the wall where many tools hung in places marked by spray-painted silhouettes. "I want you at the wedding. No excuses."

"Yeah . . ? Thanks. I guess I can. Why not?" As the words came out of my mouth I started thinking about the possible makeup of the other guests. "Not gonna be too many old characters, is there? I mean, one sight of me and a lot of these East Enders'll wanna eat nails and spit on the ground, so to speak."

"No problem. It's gonna be real cool. Classy. That's why I want you to come . . . "

"Aw . . . "

"No, really. In fact, if it hadn't been for you, I might never have got here." Danny banged at something with a hammer. A piece of chrome fell off the front of the car.

"Geez . . . Don't get mushy on me, Dan."

"Just be there," said Danny Speller, hitting something else that was loose.

The big date came fast and there I was, walking up wide stairs and going in under an arched doorway. The church was almost empty. I knew I wasn't early, I'd cut it as fine as I could. But I couldn't believe the sparseness of the turnout. Only about twenty-five people or so. I'd always heard these Chinese do's were extensive.

The service went smoothly and Danny got married to a pleasant-looking Chinese girl, small even for her race. People stood around the doorway shaking hands.

I was introduced to the father of the bride as a respected friend of the groom. Shaking the man's hand, I sighted over his shoulder, some distance away, a lovely woman, silk-clad, talking to the bride. I could see even from there the beauty of her face. It was striking, distinctive, but neither all Asian or white or otherwise. Perfectly ambiguous. I thanked the father of the bride, Mr. Chee, for having me.

Driving away, I tried to get another look at the silk-woman, but she'd ducked into some car or other.

v v v

The reception was being held in a big Dim Sum place downtown. The parking lot was full and I had to drive around the block twice to get a spot on the street. A hand-painted sign on the door said: Closed For Private Party. I knocked, got no answer, pulled it open and climbed stairs toward the second floor. A jungle of voices wafted down as I got higher. At the top the room was packed with people, scads of them. A heavy, thick-armed type stood sucking a beer near the reception desk at the top of the stairs. The can looked like a miniature in his hand. "This the Chee party?" I asked.

"Yeah, man. Who are you?"

"A friend," I said, looking around.

Despite the brusqueness of his greeting, I decided to be pleasant and faced the man squarely, offering my hand. "Barry Delta's the name." Now that I looked at him he seemed familiar.

"Barry! So it's true. You are coming to Danny's wedding."

"Yeah . . . . George, isn't it?"

"Georgie Bains. Remember? My second bit for robbery. You were my PO."

"Oh, yeah . . . "

"Haven't seen you in five years. How you been doin'?"

"Okay, I guess. You?"

"Great. Been driving truck for the last coupla years. Back and forth to California. Me an' the ol' lady got a place in Surrey, right. Fourteen-wide mobile. Own the whole thing ourselves, eh." Georgie hoisted the beer and took a healthy pull. "'S the only way to go."

"Well," I said, "good to see you behaving yourself and staying out of trouble."

"Oh, I wouldn't say that! Hah, hah . . . "

Georgie drank again. I looked around.

"Danny and the bride here yet?"

"Naw, they're doin' pictures. Danny wants me to watch the door and sorta be a bouncer. I guess it's okay to let you in. Ha, ha!"

"Thanks." I stepped to the side, peering over the crowd. "Guess I'll go find a drink."

"Go ahead." Georgie Bains stood aside to let me through, but his face darkened before I passed. "Say, look, if it's no trouble. I kinda want to talk to you about my cousin. Wayne Stickner. You know him."

"Wayne? Sure. He's your cousin?"

"On my mom's side."

"What's it about?"

"He's kinda screwed up."

"That's not hard to see."

"It's tough, seein' him sitting in the joint like that . . . "

"He beat up a store clerk. What can I say?"

"There's good reasons for what he did."

"I guess . . . . Maybe, in some twisted kind of way. But that doesn't change anything . . . "

"Yeah, well . . . We can't talk now. I'll catcha later . . . "

"Fine . . . ." I eased around Georgie and away.

∨ ∨ ∨

There were a multitude coming up the stairs. The place would soon be impossibly packed with people. I moved into the restaurant, not looking at anybody directly, for fear of recognition. The party was well under way. Easily about a hundred people, at it hard. There were large round tables set for ten each, all of them with bottles of liquor: whisky, rum, gin, vodka . . . anything you want. Most of the guests looked like they'd been "wanting" a lot.

I found a table that looked like it hadn't been disturbed and broke the seal on a bottle of scotch. I almost had a healthy shot poured by the time the first Hey, Barry! went off. Across the floor I recognized another one of my all-stars, pointing to me, red-faced and inebriated-looking. This I did not need. I got up, drink in hand, pretending I hadn't heard, and made for another part of the room.

I began to see the crowd in something like a total perspective, sitting and standing around, drinking and getting sweaty-uncomfortable in good clothes and the occasional tie. Most of the ethnic and territorial youth gangs in the city were represented. On one side, the Commercial Drive Italian contingent, swearing and speaking among themselves in a male huddle, ignoring their women. At another place the mixed-bag caucasian muddle of the Clark Park gang, tattoos and knife wounds grinningly displayed. In the back of the room, looming, were the quiet-hostile Golden Leopards, an unsmiling, non-talking bunch of lean Vietnamese toughies glaring with cruel eyes.

Then I saw her. Across the floor, sitting at a table with an elderly lady. Both looked uncomfortable. I took a slug of my drink, wondering what to do. The place was getting even more packed. The noise level was as high as it can get without music playing. Drunken voices were starting to rise above the general din, like piccolo strains dancing out over the tubas.

I looked around, plotting my course over to her table. Georgie Bains had torn himself from doorman duty and was slugging healthily at a beer. He wiped his mouth and saw me. I turned, but too late. He was already moving. I got going, side-slipped behind a big group of people standing in a circle and tried to look invisible. A couple of hulking loud-talkers got in Georgie's way and spoke, distracting him. I skipped past the quiet Vietnamese and it was home free to her table. I saw with approval that the old woman with her was sitting somewhat away from her, out of earshot.

She had what the romance novelists call an imperious manner. She watched my approach without seeming to use her eyes. By the time I was at her table, I still didn't have an opening line. I decided to go with logic.

"You don't belong here," I said.

"Brilliant. I knew I'd meet a rocket scientist sooner or later."
She spoke looking away, in a voice of precise velvet.

"Name's Barry Delta."

"Barry Delta. Kind of a geometrical ring to it."

"Oh?"

"I always disliked geometry."

All I could do was grin slightly, catching her tone. I forged ahead.

"Me too."

She finally looked at me. Her eyes told a history of boredom.

"My name is Ming. Do you have a car?"

"Right outside."

She looked sidelong at the boisterous crowd.

"Do you have any vested interest in staying longer?"

"Nothing vested. The guy's a friend of mine, he's my mechanic. You?"

"The bride is my cousin. We'd never met before today."

"Bad place to start an acquaintance . . ."

"Look, I'm desperate to get out of here. Will you take me?"

"Okay. Let me find the boys' room. I'll be right back."

She smiled then, the first time I'd seen her do it, a radiant kiss from the sun. The scotch had hit bottom. I didn't know if it was the booze or if it was her. My face went hot, like looking into a gas-fed bonfire. I hoped it didn't show. I belted down the rest of my drink.

"Don't be long," she said. "I can't sit here looking tough forever."

"Hold fast. They only eat their own, generally. Unless you get between them and the booze . . ." I tore my eyes away from her and looked around the room. There were too many people and too much noise. Some of the characters were going booze-stupid. Ugliness was on its way. The best thing would be to vanish immediately. Especially with the company I'd acquired. "Just hurry," she said.

The washrooms were at the back, I pressed through as unobtrusively as possible, avoiding direct looks at anybody. The

151

men's room door opened sluggishly, many people were inside, leaning against walls. I edged over to the troughs and unzipped, noticing a couple of giggling girls off in one corner. Modesty be damned. They were busy snorting milk sugar up their noses, pretending to snap fresh, otherwise occupied. I faced the urinal, and hoped I could make water with all the room's possible drama fusing off at my back.

Thankfully, I did. Finishing up, I started hearing pieces of conversation. The Vietnamese and the Italians were having a debate:

"Like fuck," someone said. "Pizza brains don't got da balls, right?"

"Somethin' else, zipper-head," said a thick voice. "Try 'em out right now, eh?"

The two scrappers, a thick, black-haired Commercial Drive espresso-sweater and a mean-looking, thin-limbed Boatperson stared each other down, not paying attention. A drunken Doug Park thug, tattoos rippling, approached to make a third. "What kinda fuckin' deal is this, man?" he slurred.

Before anyone could answer, another fellow stepped up and spat: "Shut the fuck up and go feed your pit bull!" Whereupon, the first punch got thrown.

In a second, I saw the glint of metal in the Italian's hand. From out of sight in a stall, a black-slippered foot appeared, kicking upward. The move of a much-practiced kick-boxer it must have been, for the foot rose much above the heads of both glarers, and neatly removed the knife from out the Italian's hand to send it point-first into the acoustic ceiling tile. For a second everyone except the fighters at the door gazed in wonderment at the stuck-hard knife, a bone-white shiny switch-blade, the kind so easy to buy in Mexico.

The girls in the corner grabbed each other and fled into a stall. Movements for position were made. Figures blurred in my vision, sideways-walking as I was toward the door. I hoped that a black form clutched in someone's hand off in a corner wasn't what I thought it was. I grabbed the door handle and pulled hard, stepped out and flung the door back. No Uzi bullets. Breathing heavily, I lunged away, only to be stopped, staring into the angry, beer-reddened eyes of Georgie Bains.

"Been lookin' for you, Delta. You fucked my little cousin over. We gotta settle . . ."

"Gladly," I said, moving aside. "In here . . ."

With me holding the door, Georgie dutifully stepped into the washroom, tripped over a body and fell into the fray. I slipped out, stuffing the door quickly shut.

The crowd, oblivious to the men's room business, stood thickly immobile. Ming had her coat around her shoulders and stood up as soon as she saw me.

"Quick, one of the Vietnamese looks like he's going to make a move on me. Where's your car?"

"Out front."

We made our way. The fun in the washroom seemed not to have spread; the din from the crowd was more than enough to cover the noise.

Then the wedding party arrived, rising from the stairwell like cake-top figures riding up on a conveyer belt. The moms and dads were close behind. They stood at the top of the stairs, looking around. Few noticed them. A couple of girls ran to the bride.

"Barry!" cried Danny when he saw me.

"Hi Dan . . ."

I couldn't say anything more because of the loud breaking sound of the men's room door as it exploded off its hinges. The crowd hushed slightly and turned its attention to the ruckus. Danny looked past my shoulder to see what was the matter.

I could feel the action approaching. Grabbing Ming's hand, I eased past the wedding party. "Sorry, gotta go . . ." A chair hit the wall not far away. We hurried down the stairs to the quiet street.

v v v

We strode, still holding hands.

"I hope the night isn't a total loss for you," she said. The quiet of the street did wonderful things for her already glorious voice.

"Don't worry."

"Where's your car?"

We were almost there, I found the keys and pulled them out.

"Be it ever so humble," I said, stopping at the Honda. "Here it is."

Ming looked at the battered, sorry-looking car, giggled, looked at me, stopped giggling.

"You're serious."

"Deadly."

Ming smiled benevolently, but her manner had changed. She disengaged her hand from mine.

"Look, I'm going to get a cab."

"Come for some dessert or something."

"Really. I must get back."

"I'll take you."

"There's no point. I really couldn't impose . . . "

She turned.

"You're sure?" No answer. She walked quickly, high-heels clicking. I watched for a while. Then, because it felt better to talk to myself than to stand alone in the silence, I said: "You're not so sure."

v v v

(One of Barry's letters, subsequent to Janice)

> *By now it's been too long since we spoke. I know you enough, you'd rather be on speaking terms. I definitely would. I need to tell you about myself, as if you didn't know. I need to tell you. I need a lot. I try to get by on less. It doesn't work. I miss you. I struggle with what would be the proper*

154

thing to do to make things right and not hurt you or set up expectations that would eventually hurt you. No clearly definable thing emerges . . . . As undeserving as I may be, I would like to hear from you . . .

(And on it went . . .)

After two years flinging the futile paper into the void, Barry gave up.

There were times when his desperation cleared, and he regretted writing, hoped she wouldn't respond. Whatever his mood, he was always disappointed with himself.

12

*We see that the caseworker is vulnerable to emotional
haunting by images of too many things gone askew, too many
situations gone out of control and costing lives, pain and
mental damage. He may be acutely plagued by the persistent
pictures of his more catastrophic casework disasters: a
grievously mutilated woman, alive, breathing shallowly in a
hospital bed. The laughter of a madman resonates in the
brain and may not completely go away, even when drunk or
under the influence of other drugs.*

— *Prof. Prosyst, p. 278.*

Darryl Penny's mother was a frightened woman; she
quivered, fearing. It seemed to be her natural state. Barry Delta
tried all his usual conversation tricks to make her relax.

"Nice apartment you got here. Nice view. Nice cat. Nice plants.
In fact, nice little world you have here . . . "

Mrs. Penny's smile was only an acknowledgement. She seemed
not to have been listening to what Barry said. "Yes . . ." she said
tentatively.

"Guess we might as well get down to business. Your son's
coming out next month."

"Is it that soon?" The smile, what there was of it, faded.

"Right. Pretty close." Barry read from a file. "The twenty-eighth. He says he's coming to live with you."

"Well, yes . . . I guess so."

"You don't seem very positive."

"Well . . . . He has no place to go."

"Just the same, he doesn't have to come here. You don't have to live with him if you don't want to."

"But . . . he's going to anyway. What can I do?"

"You can tell him he can't."

"Oh . . ."

"You can tell him your place is too small. You're too busy. You can't afford to feed him. Tell him anything. Tell him your cat doesn't like him. Tell him the truth . . ."

"Oh . . . I couldn't do that."

"Why not?"

"He just wouldn't like to hear that. I couldn't say that to him."

"He wouldn't listen? If that's it, don't worry. I can encourage him in that area . . ."

"Oh, it's not that. He just wouldn't hear it, you know? He would turn his head away until I finished talking and then turn back as if I hadn't said a thing and just go on talking like before. You know?"

"I think I do, yeah . . ."

Mrs. Penny's apartment was on the twelfth floor. From where he sat Barry could see out the glass doors, over the next building and the town and to the river. There was a tugboat, labouring in the murky water, towing a scow full of gravel. Barry looked back at Mrs. Penny.

"Has Darryl lived with you before, Mrs. Penny?"

"Off and on."

"Do you know what he's doing time for?"

"Something about bad cheques."

"That's partly right. You don't know what else?"

"He's been in trouble a lot. Since he was thirteen. I've lost track."

Barry thumbed through the file, found the document he was looking for and looked the woman in the eyes. "I'm going to read you your son's criminal record. This is sort of against the rules, kind of a violation of his right to privacy. But I'll risk a lawsuit here because I think you should know this stuff. Okay?"

Mrs. Penny avoided Barry Delta's gaze. "Fine," she said.

"In only three years as an adult, Darryl has racked up, let's see, five, six, seven, eight . . ." Barry turned a page. "Eleven criminal convictions. He's been charged a whole bunch more times but beat all those. It looks like usually by pleading guilty to one and having the rest dropped, getting a deal. He's presently doing three years, six months on charges of fraud, uttering, robbery, possession of stolen property, common assault, assault causing bodily harm, assaulting a peace officer and threatening. Lucky he's young. I've seen guys do fifteen years on stuff like this . . ."

Mrs. Penny's attention had turned to the window. She seemed, as Barry finished, to be watching the same tug he had been. "Most of that happened while he was living with his father," she said.

"Well, anyway . . . Darryl's a young guy. I'd like to see him stay out of jail. I'll do all I can but I could use your help."

"How could I help?"

"Just let me know, once in a while, how he's doing. I mean, it's hard for me to figure a lot of the time how things are going from just talking to a guy. I need an inside assessment of things."

"And how will I do that?"

"Here's my card. Call me anytime. I'll be coming around to visit sometimes and you can talk to me then. Or we can get together other times when he's not around if you don't want to talk in front of him. I prefer it the other way, though, with you just coming straight out and saying what's on your mind with all of us here. Shakes things loose. It may feel bad at the time, but it's better for everybody in the long run. Get things worked out. Don't let things build up."

Mrs. Penny turned back from the window. "You mean right in front of him?"

"Sure."

Barry realized, holding out his card, that this woman had never done such a thing. Never thought about it. He imagined, from her wide-eyed stare, that she might consider him a fool for suggesting it.

"Okay . . . " Mrs. Penny took Barry's card gingerly in her hand, staring at it, wary, as if it might burn her. "If you say so . . . "

Leaving, Barry took one last stab. "Even before he gets out, if you have second thoughts, if you want to talk about anything, feel free to call. Just pick up the phone . . . "

"Fine," she said.

Barry knew she wouldn't call, ever, by the scared look in her eyes.

A nervous, wiry little fellow, Darryl Penny had earned most of his assault convictions for resisting arrest while under the liberating influence of any number and/or combination of intoxicating agents. Within two hours of his release, with three Serax-10's in his bloodstream, he stepped into Barry Delta's office and sat on the edge of a chair. Downers or no, he was still a jumpy, nervous little man.

"I spoke with your mother," Barry said after the introductions.

"I know," said Darryl. "You guys allowed to do that?"

"What, speak to the family? Of course . . . "

"No, I mean tell her all that. Get her all worried. She doesn't have to know all the stuff I'm s'posed to have committed."

"Oh. Sorry. I felt like she should know. Don't you?"

"No."

"Oh. So we disagree . . . "

"Look, Mr. Delta. I don't want no trouble. You want me to come in here and talk to you I'll come in and talk. But leave her out of it, okay? I mean, what's she got to do with it, anyway?"

"I don't know. She probably knows you better than anybody. Don't you think your mother probably knows you better than anybody?"

"Not necessarily."

"Hmmm . . . . You got a girlfriend?"

"No."

"See much of your dad?"

"Naw."

"Well, we're getting pretty lean on sources, here. You got any close friends?"

"Not around here."

"Well, I'd say that does it. Your mother is elected to be the one who knows you best. Outside of yourself, of course."

"Yeah, maybe . . . . Look, ah . . . can I go now? I mean, isn't this about enough for today?"

"You just got here. Why so jumpy?"

"I'm not jumpy."

"You're nervous as a cat. Loosen up. Use more of that chair, sit back and relax. Tell me about yourself . . . "

"You already know. You got all kinds of files and stuff."

"Other people's words. Give me yours."

Darryl edged even closer to the lip of his chair, all but falling off. Barry sensed him seizing up, in a clench of fear. The look on his face read plainly. It said: Why does this have to happen to me? All my life people have been asking for things I can't deliver. What do you want, anyway? Whatever it is, I can't give . . .

"I . . . I always find it hard to talk about myself," he said, quivering.

"Problem number one." said Barry Delta.

Two weeks went by without word from Darryl. Barry Delta was not surprised. For some reason, even though this was not an unusual case—God knows lots of other parolees disappeared after the first meeting—Barry had trouble controlling a basic anger

160

about the thing. Something in Darryl Penny's manner, something about his mother's attitude, something about the whole stupid set-up riled Barry in a way he couldn't understand. Stress. Barry looked forward to the week's vacation he had coming up. He could hardly wait.

v v v

"Hello, Darryl?"

"Who's this?"

"That any way to answer a phone? It's Delta. Your PO. Remember?"

"Oh. Yeah. Okay, yeah . . . Howya doin'?"

"That's not important. The important thing is how are you doing?"

"Okay."

"I don't think so. You must have been sick or something. On your deathbed. Nearly killed in a car accident . . . "

"Huh . . . ?"

" . . . Nothing short of it to have kept from calling me ten days ago like you were told."

"Oh . . . "

"So tell me, how you been doing? Really."

"Hey, y'know, other guys don't have to call their PO's every three days. How come I have to?"

"You're special, Darryl."

"Yeah, sure . . . "

"I'm concerned. Not just about you but about your mother. How's it working out, you living with her?"

"Okay."

"Okay . . . Seems to be kind of a stock answer with you . . . "

"What?"

"Never mind. Stick around. I'm coming over."

"What . . . now?"

"Yeah, now. What's the matter, you got plans?"

161

"No, but . . ."

"Half an hour, I'll be there."

Something was up, Barry could feel it. He gunned the Honda across town and got to Darryl's place in twenty minutes.

v v v

"Darryl," Barry said when the apartment door opened, "what the hell's going on?" He walked into the apartment, looking for Mrs. Penny. "Where's your mother?"

"She's . . . taking a shower." Darryl pointed to the closed bathroom door. "Nothing's going on. Honest."

Barry looked closely at the door, walked slowly by, and saw a line of light showing under it. He heard the sputter of the shower being turned on.

In the living room, Darryl sat in a chair and fidgeted with a pack of cigarettes. Several half-smoked butts lay in an ashtray.

Barry sat in the middle of the sofa and dug his hands down into his jacket, looking at Darryl closely. "What's the matter?" he asked.

"Nothing."

"Why the nerves? You're sprung like a slug on a salt-lick."

"Forget it. Just nerves, that's all . . . "

"For god sakes, Darryl! If something's eating you tell me about it. It's your only chance. Let yourself get weird and do something dumb and it's back to the joint for you. Simple. Get that through your head."

"Yeah?" Anger rose. Darryl stopped playing with the cigarettes and stared at Barry. "And you'd do it too, wouldn't you?"

"Whoa. Hold on. That's not the idea at all. I'm trying to get you through this thing, not hold you back. Where'd you get a crazy idea like that? You don't know me well enough to know how I act."

"You guys are all the same."

"Nope. That's an insult, boy. Watch your tongue."

"Well, maybe you're okay, but sooner or later you run into somebody on a power trip. I don't want any a that kinda shit. Just wanna do my time . . ."

"Now that's what I like to hear. And I'm the man to help. Anything bothers you, you just tell me and I'll do what I can to smooth things over. Cops hassling you?"

"Nope."

"Guys from the joint? Anybody come around?"

"Nope. Nobody knows I'm here."

"Smart way to play it."

"I figured that would be best."

"See? You're already doing things right. Looked for work?"

"Well, not really."

"What's the matter?"

"I dunno. Guess I'm still on a party."

"You've had two weeks. Party's over. What kind of work do you do when you do it?"

"I don't know . . . anything, I guess. Washed dishes once. Worked at a gas station . . ."

"Sit tight. I'll look into something for you. I got a connection at a car wash. You wanna work at a car wash?"

"I dunno. Guess it would be alright."

"Sit tight. I'll give you a call by tomorrow. Might want you to go downtown and talk to a guy. Be at your best . . ."

"Right . . ."

"Good man . . ."

Though things were going better, Barry still received panic messages from Darryl. His fidgeting had resumed. Although he had not, as Barry had expected he immediately would, lit a cigarette, he still played with the pack. From where he sat, Barry could faintly hear the shower water still going.

"Your mom takes long showers."

"Yeah."

"You told her I was coming . . . ?"

"Oh, yeah . . . "

Just then the shower stopped. Barry was glad. He was intent on at least seeing Mrs. Penny, to check for damage. The state of this family, you never knew. Barry had seen physical abuse in a parent-to-child direction, but would not have been surprised at an opposite situation here. Though, when he thought about it, Darryl may be a lot of things, but he didn't come across as the mother-beater type. But you never knew. Their basic dispositions being what they were, maybe they took turns sitting around scaring each other. Barry waited, petting the cat, making idle conversation, for Mrs. Penny to get out of the bathroom.

"Nice view from here, huh?"

"Huh?" Darryl had hypnotized himself momentarily with the cigarette pack. "Yeah, I guess. Look, if that's all, I gotta go."

"Always in a hurry . . . "

"Well, it's been a long time. Still getting used to being out . . . "

"I guess you're allowed . . . "

"Good."

"Just don't go too fast. Life lasts a lot longer than you sometimes think. It only goes fast when you're having too much fun . . . "

"Yeah . . ?"

"That's my philosophy, anyway. Take it or leave it. Cheap at the price . . . "

"Uh huh . . . . Guess so. Thanks."

"Well, I guess I'll get going . . . " Barry got up to go. "Now I've told you all I know, don't forget what I said."

"Yeah . . . "

"Any trouble, crack to me. It's important. You may not think so, but it is."

"Yeah . . . "

Walking down the hallway, toward the door, Barry heard the shower water go on again. Something was far-wrong, beyond all control. He could feel it in the air like a bad smell. It was one of those times when something wonderful had to be conjured, some

164

magic-wise thing said that would shake loose all the clumsy deceit going on and bare the truth like an opened clam. But nothing was coming to Barry. He slowed by the bathroom door and almost leaned close to hear better. The water was rushing.

He thought of calling out to Mrs. Penny. He knew, whatever his instincts, that this might simply be the case of a woman who did not want to talk to him, had her reasons, certainly had her rights, maybe even typically took two consecutive showers in the same hour out of long-established habit. Who knows. All Barry knew was that there was something amiss here, something undoubtedly significant, and he did not know what that something was. He needed help. Badly. Even just a little. But he wasn't getting it.

He stopped by the hallway, turned to Darryl and said, as firmly as he could, "What's going on?"

"Nothin's going on!"

"YES THERE IS! YES THERE FUCKING WELL IS! Where the hell is your mother? I want to speak to her right now."

"She's in the fuckin' shower! You want me to drag her out here with no clothes on? You into that kinda shit, Delta?"

Barry moved to the bathroom door, brushing past Darryl.

"Shut your mouth, punk, or I'll sling your ass back in stir just to brighten my fucking day, if you get my drift. Mrs. Penny! You in there?"

v v v

In the bathroom, fully clothed and quivering, Mrs. Penny sat on the toilet lid, staring in a daze. She had a black eye. The shower water ran, creating steam.

She winced at the pounding on the door. She could clearly hear Barry call: "Mrs. Penny! Are you alright?"

"I'm fine," she said quietly.

"MRS. PENNY!"

"Fine. I'm fine!"

v v v

On the other side of the door, Barry pounded again, fueled by anger. Darryl stood off, arms folded, glowering.

Barry called again. "Are you alright in there?"

"I'm fine. Go away."

"What?"

"Go AWAY! WE DON'T NEED YOU!"

Barry stepped back from the door.

Darryl sniffed. "See?"

"No, I don't see. I don't see a thing. Maybe I should, but I don't."

Barry glanced once more at the bathroom door, then moved to leave.

At the door, Barry said: "Tell your mother I want to talk to her. Nothing's right until she does."

"Okay," said Darryl, already closing the door.

This happened on a Wednesday. The next day, Thursday, Barry tried twice to phone Darryl and his mother but got no answer. Friday was a busy day, mainly because Barry wanted to leave early and nothing would stop him. A plane ticket to San Francisco burned in his pocket. His bags were packed and in the car. He'd be there in time for late dinner at his favourite North Beach bistro. He could taste the veal parmigiana already, and his first shot of good, cheap bourbon. He flashed through the day like aluminum foil, cutting corners. He forgot about Darryl Penny.

Another thing Barry forgot was his regular browsing of the city police bulletins, accumulated for the week and sitting atop the filing cabinets in the back of the office. You never knew who you might see in them. Barry considered it fun to go through and find out who was getting arrested where and what for. It was not infrequent Barry would find one of his old success stories once more stepping over the line. Other times he would be alarmed to see one of his current charges nabbed for crimes as yet not fully investigated, and hurry down to the police station to get the story.

If he'd stuck around this Friday afternoon, Barry would have seen a bank-camera photograph and recognized immediately the frightened face of the "Baseball Bandit" so named for his habit of robbing banks with a Vancouver Canadians cap pulled low over his face. But Barry wouldn't have mistaken Darryl Penny's naked fear under ten baseball caps. He would have issued warrants, called police and had Darryl back safely in prison in a matter of hours.

But this did not happen, and for the next seven days Barry had a hell of a good time in San Francisco. He dined on Italian food every night, drank and sang in the bars, slept late and wandered museums and art galleries in the afternoons. He went to the Legion of Honour museum, contemplated Rodin, and was much taken with "The Thinker"; wondering why, seeing it for real in the cool bronze, this figure meant so much to him. During the tour, Barry talked to a good-looking girl who said she was a medical student from Salt Lake City. Barry often heard that people from there were awfully polite, and this girl was no disappointment. They chatted and toured, toured and chatted, sat in the coffee shop drinking mineral water and later walked out to look one last time at "The Age of Bronze".

The statue virtually spoke to Barry. He felt he knew or maybe somehow *was* the male figure—holding or touching his head, thinking or crying. He looked at the girl. No one ever looked as beautiful to him. He wondered how he might draw her closer, he thought of maybe touching her hand . . .

v v v

Near the moment that Barry contemplated reaching for the girl's hand, Darryl Penny woke from a druggy stupor with bad thoughts in his head. He lay in the wreckage of a sullen party. There were people asleep in other rooms. Darryl checked some jackets laying around and got car keys, went outside and found the one they fit.

Woozy from the dope, Darryl gunned the car down a street and up the next, desperate to go, uncertain where to. He drove around until he saw a police car and panicked and gunned the car through a busy intersection on a busy street, disregarding the light. He entered the intersection just as a young man and his wife drove across on their way home from work. Their seven-year-old daughter, just picked up from day care, was in the back of the car, strapped in and playing with her Cabbage Patch doll. Darryl Penny, his eyes red with panic at a police car that was not even following him, had not even noticed him, screamed through the red light and rammed the car broadside.

The couple, the man especially, sustained massive injuries and had to be cut out of the mangled car with The Jaws of Life. The little girl was dead. Crushed in the metal so badly her mother did not know her.

A policeman dragged Darryl from behind the wheel of his wrecked stolen car. Though bloodied about the forehead, Darryl was relatively unhurt. He sobbed like a baby.

"Why does this stuff always happen to me?"

"Shuddup!" said the policeman.

Another policeman approached from the direction of the family's car. His face was set and grim. Without a word he strode to Darryl and slapped him hard across the face. Darryl wailed.

v v v

At the moment Darryl Penny got slapped, stumbling to his knees in the intersection back home, the beautiful girl from Salt Lake City deftly withdrew her hand, smiling ever so politely at Barry Delta.

v v v

"So," said John, "Wrote it up yet?" He sat back in his chair, slipping a half-smoked cigarillo from between his lips. Barry stood immobile in his office doorway, staring.

"Wrote it up? I haven't even figured it out . . ."

"What's to figure?"

"Don't know. Why, I guess. And me. What did I have to do with it."

"You . . ?"

"I know what *they* did. I know what Penny did. His mother, I don't know, maybe it's what she didn't do. But what should I have done?"

Smoke leaked from John's nose and the gaps between his yellowing teeth. "What did you do?"

"I dunno. Tried to figure things and didn't do a good job."

"Bound to happen . . ."

"I know . . ."

" . . . All the time."

"Damn, I hope not."

"Nobody ever knows, Barry." John leaned forward, his chair creaked under the weight. "You can't ever know for sure."

"I'll never lay down for that."

"You'll never get any rest."

"How can I just let it go? I mean, something's got to result here . . . it happens too many times."

"I didn't say let it go. I said you can't predict. That's something else. But sure as hell you can do something after. It's not over."

"It isn't?"

"What are ya? Dead or something? You're still thinking about it. You hurt about it. It's not over."

"Thanks a lot. I just go on hurting."

"There's always that. But you can do something about it. Just let your mind clear for awhile . . ."

"Oh, I wish for that . . ."

"Use your imagination. Let your head run wild. Think of what *should* happen."

"What should happen . . . "

"Right . . . "

"As opposed to what *did* happen . . . "

"No, no, that's past. We're looking for a conclusion here. Something to happen now that brings the big picture into focus or somehow puts the right finish on it . . . "

"What will happen . . . . What could happen . . . "

"Right . . . "

"What should happen . . . "

"You never know about these things," said John, slipping the cigarillo back in his mouth.

Barry Delta drove through town and out into the countryside. The bad taste in his mouth would not go away and talking to Darryl Penny on the phone that afternoon had not helped matters. Darryl was in a maximum security induction cell at his old home penitentiary until the Parole Board and the courts decided what to do with him.

"What happened?" Barry had asked.

"I dunno, I guess I got kinda mixed up . . . " Barry tried not to hear the whiny, "poor me" sound in the voice. He tried to imagine it was there because of the facial injuries. Maybe there was medication, too. He tried to give Darryl more credit as a way of giving himself more credit. How can you talk to such a worm? He's not a worm. Everybody has reasons, often damn good ones, for the way they act. "Now I'm all screwed up," whimpered Darryl. "I dunno what to do . . . "

"Relax. Don't worry about decisions. You haven't got any choices. You're in a shitload of trouble . . . "

Darryl moaned long and pitifully, then blubbered: "I dunno why this kinda stuff has to happen to me. And my face is all banged up and they won't gimme anything for it. It hurts . . . "

Barry hung up the phone. By rights, he was supposed to go out and do a formal post-suspension interview. That wouldn't happen today. He tried to call Mrs. Penny. The phone rang and rang. He could feel her listening to it. He could see the fear on her face. He could not help slamming the phone down and cursing: "Yeah, fucking predictable!" Afterwards, he thought more about it. What would he say to her? Nothing much.

Barry pulled into the parking lot and drove through the paved section with the VIP spots to the gravel patch for visiting case workers.

At the gate, the guard on duty looked at Barry's signature in the sign-in book and said immediately: "I know what you're here for. You want to see that child-murdering little motherfucker we got sitting in induction." There was mirth in the man's voice. Also raw hate and just a little pity. His boldly-spoken words bounced off the clean tile walls and floor like bones clacking on stone.

"No," Barry said. "Population. I'm expected."

"Okay."

Barry walked out of the guard post, through several electric gates, down a path to the visits and socialization building, through the covered visiting area, out the open doors to the yard and sat down on one of the picnic tables set aside for inmates with families who brought food. There was no visiting at this time of day. Barry had the place to himself. Steve appeared after five minutes, looked at Barry with mild surprise, and wordlessly sat down beside him. He spoke softly at the ground: "Well, well . . . "

"Hi, Steve. Howya been?"

"Oh, sixty/forty . . . "

"Never understood what that meant. I take it you're okay, generally."

"No complaints."

"Good. Sorry again about the south-of-the-border business."

"Aw, it was my fault."

"I have to say, I sure appreciate how quiet you've been. I never heard, what did you get?"

"Nothing for the truck. Two years for the gun. Doesn't even show. But five consecutive for the robbery-assault."

"Five years? Not bad. And for assault with a weapon, yet. Quite a kiss . . ."

"Yeah, nice judge . . ."

"So you'll be out in . . . what? Three more years . . . ?"

"I done almost two now, so about three more I guess . . . "

"That's great . . ."

"Yeah, I guess . . . "

Barry was glad to see there were no hard feelings.

"So," Steve said, pulling a wrinkled cigarette pack from a shirt pocket. "You gonna be my PO again when I get out?"

"If you want. Whatever you want. But that's not why I'm here. I got a bad situation going . . ."

"Not trying to snafu another broad this time, are you? I heard about that action you had with Bertie Finwell."

"No. Nothing like that."

"Good. They're not worth it, man."

"I'm still working on that. That's a tough one. No. This thing's a personal number and I'm going to suggest several things to you. You alone. Because you're the type of individual who would know what to do in such a situation. In terms of delicacy, this is far heavier than before."

"Uh huh. Before we go any further, let's walk."

"Good idea."

The two men got up from the picnic table and began a slow wander into the middle of the exercise field. Steve stopped, stooped to idly pick at a clump of grass and looked up at Barry.

"I'll tell you right now. I'm not interested in hearing anything that doesn't have a prize on it. Understand?"

"Got it. I haven't got much, but name your price once you hear it and maybe we can move. I don't know, I hadn't thought . . ."

"I'm not being a dink or anything. I mean, it's only fair . . . "

"Oh, absolutely. Don't apologize. In fact, it just came to me. I'll offer, just for listening, my sympathetic control of your case when you get out. Every effort possible, and some not so possible. Just for listening. If you go for it, we'll talk."

"That's fair . . . "

"Good. Now I want to tell you about a guy and see if you know him. He's very nervous, no friends, no class. He's here, but not in population yet. Killed a kid with a car . . . "

"Think I got him . . . "

" . . . Guess he'd have a bandaged face or scars or . . . "

"Got him."

"Good. I don't think he's got friends. Not the type. But anyway, I've got bad things in my head about this guy and I truly don't think he should be comfortable. I mean, in terms of personal resources, I have fully extended myself with this guy and no good has come of it. In fact, extreme bad, if you know what I mean."

"I think I heard."

"Good, so you know what I'm talking about. Anyway, I feel strongly enough so that I'm standing here today and suggesting to you or anyone you might trust that if at all possible something should be done. Beyond the ordinary."

"Okay, I hear you. No need for anything more on that. Whattayou got?"

"Like I said before. Name it."

"Money?"

"Could be a problem. But there's time, I could work on it. What'll you need when you get out?"

"I dunno. Everything. A car . . . "

"A car . . . . You know mine?"

A smile. "Yeah."

"You can have it."

"Kinda beat, isn't it? Guy barfed in it once, I heard."

"It's been cleaned . . . "

"Not really my kind of wheels, though . . . "

"Granted. But it goes, Steve. It's all I got. 'Bout time I got a different one anyway. It's getting hard to see women with it . . . "

"You just finding that out?"

"No, but I had a bad experience lately. At least I hope it was just the car. Anyway. On that business. Can you?"

"Prob'ly . . ."

"You know somebody . . . ?"

"Prob'ly. No sense talking about it. But for your information, the man is marked anyway. We might have to get in line . . ."

"That's good to hear. Shows there's some spirit out here. All I know is I can't leave things the way they are."

"Been there."

"Actually, the man needs a legitimate reason to be scared. It sounds funny, but . . . I don't know if you know what I mean. I want to see that he gets it. Just once before he dies . . . . A really good cause to have the jitters."

"I don't think I get it. But no matter . . ."

"I'm also concerned about his mother, if you can believe it . . ."

"Whatever it's about, Barry, it doesn't matter."

"Yeah . . . you're right."

Barry turned to go.

Steve watched him closely. "You must really want this guy."

"Yes."

"You sure . . . ? 'Bout the car and all?"

Barry stopped and turned. "Everybody's gotta pay on this one." He looked Steve hard in the eye. "Everybody."

v v v

Walking back through the parking lot and onto the gravel, Barry Delta noticed the clear outline of each small rock at his feet. He felt it odd to suddenly start noticing such things. Like huge diamonds, all. He wondered what they'd feel like flung and ground and embedded into his skull. He unlocked the car door and got in, watching his hands to see if they were shaking. He wondered why he wasn't scared.

174

v v v

Instances of burnout in this population of workers is most
prevalent among those who surrender to thoughts of
uselessness and futility . . . Some research has shown that
those with imagination, and above all courage, to transcend
the bureaucratic and systematized acceptance of failure in
their jobs are those most likely to survive.

—*Prof. Prosyst, pp. 345-346.*

Darryl Penny strolled down the corridor of a six cell tier. Behind him was the thick glass of the security bubble with one guard in it. As Darryl slipped into his cell, the guard was not watching him.

From the corridor could be heard Darryl briefly screaming, then there were muffled blows. The guard in the security bubble was oblivious to the action and could not hear because of the thick glass. Other inmates strolled down the corridor, some looking in Darryl's cell as they passed, nonchalantly.

After the sounds were finished, Bertie Finwell poked his head out to check the guard in the bubble. He took one fast look and stepped into the corridor. Turning back to Darryl's cell, he said softly: "Okay."

At this signal, Wayne Stickner appeared from Darryl's cell and casually strolled down the corridor behind Bertie. They walked past the bubble and turned out of sight without the guard ever once looking in their direction.

Inside his cell Darryl lay dead on his bunk, arms splayed over his head. There was much blood and puncture markings over his upper chest. There was a crude-looking, hand-made knife protruding at a lethal angle from the base of his throat.

v v v

Wayne and Bertie filed into the shower room. Of the two shower stalls, one was occupied by Steve. As the two began disrobing, Steve turned the water off and stepped out of the shower.

"So," said Steve.

"Right," said Bertie.

"Easy as shit," said Wayne.

Bertie shook off his socks and stepped naked to the shower.

As Steve toweled off, a shout sounded from outside and a guard flashed by the doorway. Wiping, Steve said: "Much obliged."

Wayne scoffed. "Just come through with the jack."

From the shower, without the water turned on, Bertie said: "Right on."

"Relax . . . "

Wayne finished undressing and Bertie turned on the water. Wayne stepped into the shower and turned the water on. Steve finished drying off.

A guard appeared in the doorway.

"Alright you guys. Lockdown. Into your houses, right now."

The guard did not wait for the men to respond, but went away, down the corridor, issuing the same instructions to unseen others. Wayne immediately stepped out of the shower, having barely gotten wet. He picked up a towel. "So what is it? It couldn't be you. You don't give a shit. I don't give a shit. So who wanted this piece of shit done, eh?"

"Friend of ours."

"Yeah, sure," Wayne said, scoffing again.

Years later, as the wrecker came to pick up the Honda, no one noticed in it's dingy interior the dampened corner of a paper bag lagging from under the passenger seat. The car sat partly under a battered tarpaulin. It was raining and almost dark. Weeds and grass grew up through the wheel-wells and pieces of rusting equipment were strewn around. As they hooked up the hitch, there was the loud drumming of rain on the tarpaulin.

Ask No Questions.

Ludicrousity reins supreme in this house of greyness.

Barry Delta used to like greyness, the areas where one does not force oneself to seek a truth. Only a trend toward normalcy.

He recalls when he was in university; he avoided the hard sciences. The need for absolute answers offended him.

"How the fuck do we expect hard answers," he would ask, "when we don't know the context? The only reality is inward. We seem to exist in thought, on a plane which has no definition. How can hard science purport to provide answers when it rises from an unknown depth. The meaning of life hasn't been figured out yet, so how can we expect to nail ourselves down to an absolute existence?"

Others would argue back that the answers in an empirical world are sufficient to orient humankind in all spheres necessary to facilitate life, progress, and the opportunity to navel-gaze. This last activity was what Barry Delta was often accused of, when taking this line.

"Just ask the man on the street," he would say as a comeback. "He doesn't know. And well he shouldn't!"

"What an asshole," someone would always say.